We now had a clear view

"I can see something," I said. "Can you?"

"I see red hair!" Kiki gasped.

Red hair spread on the surface of the water. The cistern was not wide in circumference. The body was floating upright.

Kiki gasped again. "That hair is just like Melanie's. That can't be Melanie down there!" She turned to me, eyes wide, full of fear.

"Oh, no," Jon said, shaking his head.

"No. No. That can't be Melanie," I said. "Melanie is with Ray and Scarlett. They're out at Wrightsville Beach. I saw them leave."

Kiki heaved a huge sigh of relief. "You're right. I saw them leave too. It's just that…that's her hair color. How many people have hair that color?"

I could think of only one. Jon and I exchanged knowing glances before turning back to watch the drama below us.

The fireman lowered himself into the water. I was able to see his head but I could not see exactly what he was doing. Tying the rope around the body, I assumed.

In a minute, he was motioning to the other firemen. Then they were hauling the body out of the water. It did not take much effort; the body was very small. The body of a woman with a child's stature.

They laid her out on the sunny concrete.

"It's her," I said.

★

Previously published Worldwide Mystery titles by
ELLEN ELIZABETH HUNTER

MURDER ON THE CANDLELIGHT TOUR
MURDER AT THE AZALEA FESTIVAL
MURDER AT WRIGHTSVILLE BEACH
MURDER ON THE ICW
MURDER ON THE GHOST WALK
MURDER ON THE CAPE FEAR

Ellen Elizabeth Hunter

MURDER AT THE BELLAMY MANSION

WORLDWIDE®

TORONTO • NEW YORK • LONDON
AMSTERDAM • PARIS • SYDNEY • HAMBURG
STOCKHOLM • ATHENS • TOKYO • MILAN
MADRID • WARSAW • BUDAPEST • AUCKLAND

Recycling programs
for this product may
not exist in your area.

MURDER AT THE BELLAMY MANSION

A Worldwide Mystery/September 2010

First published by Magnolia Mysteries.

ISBN-13: 978-0-373-26722-4

Copyright © 2009 by Ellen Elizabeth Hunter.
All rights reserved. No part of this book may be reproduced
or transmitted in any form or by any means, electronic or
mechanical, including photocopying, recording or by any
information storage and retrieval system, without permission
in writing from the publisher. For information, contact:
Magnolia Mysteries, P.O. Box 38041, Greensboro,
North Carolina 27438 U.S.A.

This is a work of fiction. Names, characters, places and incidents are
either the product of the author's imagination or are used fictitiously,
and any resemblance to actual persons, living or dead, business
establishments, events or locales is entirely coincidental.

® and TM are trademarks of Harlequin Enterprises Limited.
Trademarks indicated with ® are registered in the United States
Patent and Trademark Office, the Canadian Trade Marks Office
and in other countries.

Printed in U.S.A.

A GREAT BIG THANK YOU TO SPECIAL FOLKS!

In October I held a fund-raiser at the North Carolina Association of Realtors convention in Charlotte where I sold books to raise dollars for Homes4NC, the association's non-profit charity organization. David Anderson of Pueblo CO and Faye Brock of Wilmington (my favorite realtors) sat with me and, during lulls, dreamed up plot ideas for this book. Those two have missed their calling! They should have become mystery writers.

Judge Joseph Furmick of Wake County explained about liens, foreclosures, and how assets are transferred during bank mergers and acquisitions. Joe's wife is my friend Karen Kiley, the events coordinator for the Cary Library.

Thank you to Beverly Tetterton for providing me with a copy of Diane Cobb Cashman's *The History of the Bellamy Mansion,* and for sharing her knowledge of Wilmington with me.

I could not have written this novel without the assistance and cooperation of the staff of the Bellamy Mansion Museum. A grateful thank you to the staff, the volunteers, and the directors of the Bellamy Mansion Museum and Preservation North Carolina for their tireless efforts on behalf of preserving North Carolina's extraordinary history and architectural heritage.

Books I read were: *Back With the Tide,* Memoirs of Ellen Douglas Bellamy; *The Bellamy Mansion, Wilmington, North Carolina,* Catherine W. Bishir; *The History of the Bellamy Mansion,* Diane Cobb Cashman. I visited websites too numerous to recall.

As always, my heartfelt appreciation goes to my very talented designer, Tim Doby.

Writing about a historic house with a verifiable, documented history was quite a challenge. I tried to set forth the facts correctly, and pray that my readers will forgive my errors.

Last but not least, a big thank you to you, my readers, whose enthusiasm for Ashley's adventures keeps me going.

Ellen Elizabeth Hunter

ONE

DURING ITS ONE HUNDRED and fifty year history not a single shot had been fired inside the stately Bellamy Mansion. Not during the Civil War. Not in the aftermath of the war when Wilmington, the lifeline of the Confederacy, fell to Federal forces, and a Union general requisitioned Dr. Bellamy's splendid home as a headquarters for himself and his troops. Not even during Reconstruction when lawless Carpet Baggers roamed our impoverished streets, buying up properties for pennies on the dollar.

Indeed, the only sharpshooting attempted inside the house during those troubled times of Yankee occupation was the hawking of tobacco juice into the once pristine white marble fireplaces. And most times those missed their mark.

Set on high ground above the golden Cape Fear River at the intersection of Market Street and Fifth Avenue, the splendid, white, colonnaded residence symbolized the heart and soul of Wilmington's historic district. This had been the homeplace for the large Bellamy family, where members came together to celebrate weddings and to mourn passings. In recent times, the mansion has become a museum, a favorite tourist attraction where visitors might glimpse the grandeur of gracious times gone by. Certainly not a residence you'd suspect of hosting murder and mayhem.

But on New Year's Day that was exactly what occurred. I knew nothing of the nefarious and murderous events about to unfold. I had no visions, no premonitions, no warnings from my friendly Tarot card reader.

For on the morning of New Year's Eve, I was in Pinehurst, celebrating the ninth day of my honeymoon with my new husband Jon.

"DARLING, SLOW DOWN. You're pumping too fast," I said, leaning toward Jon's ear.

The scent of Tuscany aftershave, sunshine, and the sexy aroma of clean, manly sweat wafted off his skin.

"Sorry," he murmured, a bit breathless. "Is this better?"

"Much. Much better," I replied, a bit breathless myself, but contemplating how, after nine days of honeymooning, we had learned that if we were to achieve mutual satisfaction, timing was everything.

Then sunlight glinting off his tousled blonde hair caught my eye and I thought again, as I had every day, how much I cherished this man.

"You're suddenly quiet back there, Ashley. You OK?" he asked.

"I'm perfect. Isn't this tandem bike fun? Don't you just love it? And here we are at the village."

THE CHARMING VILLAGE of Pinehurst spread before us, decked out for Christmas with greenery and red bows on lamp posts, twinkling lights and glitter. We peddled past the nineteenth-century Victorian Magnolia Inn at Magnolia and Chinquipin roads just as the noon carillon chimed from the Village Chapel. A half block from the intersection we parked our "bicycle-built-for-two" outside Theo's Taverna and strolled into the courtyard.

Jon took my hand. "Can you believe this weather?"

"The weather gods are smiling down on us," I said. "Gifting us with glorious weather for our honey-moon."

"Seventy-five degrees and here it is New Year's Eve. Let's not go inside. Let's have lunch out here in the courtyard."

"Oh, yes, let's. This will always be a special place for us. Just look at it. Fountains and statues. And all this lush landscaping."

The maître d greeted us with recognition. "Mr. and Mrs. Campbell, you have returned. I have a nice table for you two. You young lovebirds want to be alone. No?" And he seated us at an out-of-the-way corner table where we had a good view of the patio and the other diners but felt a sense of privacy. He presented us with menus. "Your server will be here shortly. And how are you enjoying our beautiful Pinehurst?"

"Couldn't be happier," Jon said. "And we've im-proved our golf games." He lied. Truth be told, we'd been too occupied with "honeymooning" to devote seri-ous time to golfing. "Next trip," Jon would say about our failure to tee-off, and then drag me back to bed. I had not protested.

Our maître d beamed benignly at us, as if he knew just what mischief we had been up to during our days. And nights. "There will be much celebration tonight. And fireworks on Pinehurst One. *Kali orex,*" he said, wishing us a good appetite.

Our server took our drink order and I requested iced tea. "At least they serve Southern tea," I said, "as well as the traditional *ouzo*."

Jon laughed. "I'm passing on the *ouzo*. I want to be sober when I start drinking champagne tonight."

"I'm having the salad," I said.

"Is that all? I'm going for the *moussaka*."

I dropped my menu onto the tabletop. "Jon, the spa not only gave me the ultimate massage, and styled my hair in the best do it's ever had, not to mention makeup, manicure and pedicure. They also weighed me on their most accurate scales. And I have gained two pounds in nine days. I'll soon have a muffin top spreading around my middle."

"Muffin top!" Jon hooted.

"Yes, a muffin top. That's a fat roll that pudges out above your waistline. Looks just like a puffy muffin top."

Jon threw back his head and laughed. "I didn't see one ounce of fat on you this morning. And believe me I looked at every inch."

My face flushed as I remembered the passion of our morning. "Well, it's there. The scales don't lie."

Our server returned with two tall, frosty glasses of iced tea. "I'll have the Greek salad," I told him. "And please bring the olive oil on the side."

"Yes, madam," he replied with old world formality.

Jon ordered the *moussaka*. Jon can eat anything and he never gains a pound. Men!

"They say a good marriage makes a woman fat," I complained. "And that is not going to happen to me."

He gave my hand a squeeze. "I won't tempt you, darling. At least not with food."

"Thanks," I said, and grinned at him. "There's plenty else for you to tempt me with."

"I already have, and you're already hooked."

I batted his hand away. "Feeling pretty sure of yourself for an old man, aren't you?" Jon is eight years older than I, thirty-four to my twenty-six, and I like to rib him about the difference.

"Sure," he laughed. "I've got exactly what you want. Be honest. Admit it."

I leaned my head over onto his shoulder. "You are everything I want. And I am so happy. I don't want this to ever end."

"It won't. We'll be on a perpetual honeymoon for the rest of our married life."

"Even when I'm hot and sweaty, covered with dirt and grime, as we climb up into the Bellamy Mansion belvedere?" I asked.

"Even then," he said with mock solemnity. "Oh, I almost forgot, Willie called to wish us a happy new year while you were in the shower."

"I'm sorry I missed a chance to tell him 'Back at ya,'" I said. Willie Hudson is the general contractor who has been working with us since we founded our restoration business.

Jon continued, "Willie plans to start work on the belvedere tomorrow morning. He's going to examine each window, chalk mark those that have to be removed. Take pictures. Assess the damage. Make notes. Then he'll discuss his findings with us when we return home on Saturday."

Jon and I had waived our fee for the work we would

do to restore the belvedere. The observatory was a local Wilmington landmark. During the fall of Ft. Fisher, a look-out had been posted in the belvedere to observe the Union Navy's bombardment on the Fort. Knowing that the Bellamy Museum was short of cash, and in a spirit of community dedication, we had volunteered our services. Willie had volunteered his work as well, and that of his crew which consisted of sons and grandsons. We would need to be reimbursed for materials and for any work contracted out, but that should be a modest reimbursement. There was never enough money to maintain historic sites.

"I've lost track of my days," I said. "It's New Year's Eve. Of course, the mansion will be closed tomorrow, New Year's Day."

"A good time for Willie to eyeball the state of disrepair," Jon said. "We're lucky to have him to start this project since it was decided right before the wedding and there was no time for us to get involved."

"Willie knows more about old house construction than you and I put together. Hands on. I hope we don't have to remove all of the windows. It's always preferable to make the repairs with the windows in place. But the project was put off for too long, and their deterioration just accelerated."

Our food arrived. Jon's *moussaka* looked tempting with its bubbling cheeses, eggplant, and beef. But I was determined to be satisfied with my salad. Good thing I love feta cheese and *kalamata* olives.

"Did you tell Willie that his nephew Brian is here?" I asked.

"No. I didn't think that was wise. You know, there is not much love lost between those two branches of the Hudson family. Some ancient family feud I guess," Jon said.

"And probably no one remembers the cause of the feud," I said. "Isn't that always the way?"

After lunch we toured the village on foot, exploring upscale boutiques and art galleries. There were many tourists in town, here for the holidays and for the excellent golfing and mild weather.

"I think we'd better get back to the hotel for a nap before it's time to dress for the party tonight," I suggested. The Carolina Hotel was hosting a New Year's Eve festivity called "Party in the Pines."

Jon wagged his eyebrows at me. "I'm getting to really like this *siesta* custom we picked up in Italy. Although there is not much sleeping involved."

I gave him a pouty look. "Well, if you want to sleep, I certainly won't do anything to keep you awake."

His eyes were dancing when he said, "Are you kidding? You'd better."

As we mounted the bike, I asked, "What time are we meeting Brian and Jackie for cocktails?"

"I told Brian we'd meet them in the bar at seven."

"Good, it'll be fun to celebrate New Year's Eve with them. Someone from home. They're such an upbeat couple. We'll just have to be careful not to tell Willie."

Brian was the son of Willie's brother Abinah. While Willie and his sons and grandsons had gone into the building trades' professions, Abinah and his line had become lawyers and politicians.

Brian Hudson was a real-estate attorney whose firm handled most of the closings for my sister Melanie, Wilmington's star realtor. Brian's wife Jackie was an environmentalist and a dedicated fund raiser for historic preservation projects which, as we liked to say, were the ultimate recycling ventures.

As we pedaled back to the hotel, I felt like pinching myself. This was all too good to be true. My life was perfect. I had married my best friend and partner, the love of my life. Our business as historic house restorers had grown quite successful. Although our motives for volunteering to restore the belvedere were altruistic, our involvement with one of North Carolina's premiere residences would produce valuable publicity and generate future business. It was indeed all too good to be true, and just a little bit spooky. How long could this streak of fine fortune last? Were we tempting the fates with our happiness?

I gave my head a shake. OK, Wilkes, lose the negative mindset. Drop it. Be thankful for your blessings and enjoy them.

As we parked our bike and walked into the stately Victorian Carolina Hotel, I said, "We'll have to coordinate our repairs on the belvedere with the Bellamy Museum's schedule. They've closed the belvedere to the tour, so we can work up there when the museum is open, but we'll have to arrange to bring tools and materials up the stairs early in the morning before they open to the public."

"They have a caretaker who comes in early to unlock the doors and clean up. But we'll set up a schedule with the site manager just as soon as we get back," Jon said, and we stepped on the elevator.

We were alone, and he gave me a quick squeeze. "Come along, young lady, this tired old man needs his bed."

BRIAN AND JACKIE HUDSON were waiting for us in the Ryder Cup Lounge. Jackie looked sleek in a sapphire blue satin sheath evening gown that was fabulous with her golden brown skin tones. Would anyone ever describe me as sleek, I asked myself. I eat too much. I like food too much. Then I have to diet to lose the extra pounds, but they have a way of creeping right back around my middle. I vowed to take it easy on the calories tonight, but that would be difficult. The cuisine here was legendary.

"Happy New Year!" the Hudsons sang out when they saw us. Brian and Jon were handsome in tuxedoes. I had on a red gown with a sheer chiffon ruffle that flared out below my knees and that would show off my legs during dancing.

The Hudsons held martinis in their hands and Jon and I ordered two for us. We found a table and settled in. Jon grabbed a handful of peanuts and not wishing to tempt me, pushed the bowl toward Brian and Jackie.

"Not for me," Jackie said. "I'm saving my appetite for better things. And Brian cannot eat peanuts."

A group near our table burst into loud laughter.

"I've got news worthy of celebrating," Brian shouted.

"Let's hear," Jon shouted back.

"Our firm has landed an important contract with Citigroup. You know, they're getting that three hundred billion dollar bailout from the government. But they're cutting staff. So they are contracting out some of the work that will be necessary to ensure they get the bailout money."

"What do you have to do?" I asked.

But the crowd was in high spirits, the bar noisy with

laughter, and I couldn't hear Brian's reply. "Later," I said. It was going to be a noisy but fun night.

At eight we went into the dining room for a four course gourmet dinner. True to my New Year's resolution, I ate small portions of the lobster bisque, filet mignon, and the sweet potato Napoleon, having lugubriously submitted my resignation to the "Clean Plate Club" for all eternity.

"Brian, tell us about the Citigroup contract?" Jon asked as a busboy cleared away our plates.

"It's all he can talk about," Jackie said with a yawn.

Brian braced his elbows on the table and leaned forward to confide, "I'm sure you've heard how the government is bailing out the big banks."

Jon and I nodded.

"Well, as a requirement to collect the funds, the banks have got to clean up their books."

"Have they been cooking the books, too?" I asked, reminded of the Enron scandal.

Brian flashed a smile. "No, that's not what I meant. They've got to clear their books of old loans. The more they can show they are cleaning up on bad debts, the more money they get.

"But..." and he paused to remove a cigar from his inside jacket pocket.

"You can't smoke in here," Jackie warned. "Save that for later. I'm sure Jon will join you outside."

Brian returned the cigar to his pocket and gave it an affectionate pat. "Sure. I'm just so excited about this big deal. As I was explaining, they're trying to clean up the old notes they've been holding, but at the same time, they are cutting staff drastically. So they've decided to outsource the collection process to various local law firms. And our firm got the job for New Hanover County. We'll trace the borrowers, enforce liens on properties, foreclose when necessary, and rake in a fat fee on what we collect."

"Are there many debtors in this situation?" I asked.

"More than you'd think. Some of the notes they've been holding are so old you'd be amazed. Even the Bellamy Mansion is involved."

"The Bellamy Mansion!" I exclaimed.

"How can that be?" Jon asked, disbelieving. We did not approve of the methods financial institutions had been using in their greedy quest for more and more money.

And I couldn't help thinking: take out liens? Foreclose? Haven't we had enough of that?

LATER, WE STROLLED into the South Room for the dessert buffet. "The food here sure lives up to its reputation," Brian said.

"I'm passing on dessert," I told Jon as we eyed the display of rich confections. "Select something chocolaty and I'll have just one bite."

"I'm skipping dessert, too," Jackie said. "I don't care for sweets."

So that was her secret for staying slim. I couldn't imagine not caring for sweets. What must that be like?

"We'll dance off the calories," Jon said.

We drifted into the Cardinal Ballroom where the Band of Oz was playing. And just as Jon promised, we danced until midnight when we raised our champagne flutes in a toast to the New Year. Everyone was kissing everyone else, and everyone was wishing everyone else a happy new year. But most importantly, I was kissing Jon.

THE NEXT MORNING we slept in. The ringing of the hotel telephone jarred us awake. Jon picked up. His voice was groggy but then he shouted, "What?" in a fully charged voice.

I sat up against my pillow and watched him as he listened. His eyes never left mine, as if he was trying to telegraph what he was hearing. "We'll be there as fast as we can."

I knew something would go wrong. I had just been thinking yesterday that things were too good to be true. Something bad had happened. To someone we cared about. But who?

"What?" I cried as he replaced the receiver. "Please tell me nothing has happened to Melanie. Tell me quick."

"It's Willie," Jon blurted. "Willie's been shot. He was up in the belvedere, working on the windows just like he said he was going to do. And someone shot him. Shot him from an upper window at the Carolina Apartments across the street."

Jon looked bewildered. I felt bewildered.

"Is he dead?" I asked faintly.

"No. No. Thank god for that. But he's in bad shape. He's having surgery right now. Come on, we've got to pack and get back home."

TWO

"WHAT A WAY TO START a new year!" Melanie wailed. Her honeymoon had been cut short, as had ours.

Jon and I had driven straight home to Wilmington to anxiously pace the floor at the medical center, in a lounge crowded with Willie's large extended family, waiting for word from the neurosurgeon who was operating on Willie's skull. Esther, Willie's wife of fifty-three years, remained an island of tranquility in a roiling sea of frantic children and grandchildren who were beset with fear that "grandpop" was going to die.

"He's gonna be fine. He's gonna be fine," she told her family repeatedly.

"How can you know that?" her grandson Dwayne asked, struggling hard to hold back his tears.

"Why the good Lord told me so," Esther declared fiercely. "Now y'all stop this bawling and you give thanks. Thanks that the good Lord sent that skilled surgeon to save your grandpa's life. That's what I'm doing. I'm giving thanks."

"And what about the sorry bastard that shot my pa?" Willie's son Mason argued. "What does the Lord tell you about why he ain't been caught?"

"Don't you show that kind of disrespect, boy," Esther said, even more fiercely than before. "You're a Christian, son, you act like one."

"Sorry, Mama," Mason said.

"He won't get away, don't you worry none about that. They'll catch him," she said.

And that settled that. Mama Hudson was never wrong.

"She's never wrong," her other son Lonnie affirmed. "If Mama says something is so, then it is so."

WE LEARNED THAT by the time the police and ambulance had arrived, in all the commotion that ensued as the paramedics squeezed their equipment up into the belvedere to work over Willie's unconscious body, and while the police calculated the trajectory of the bullet that had felled him, some thirty minutes had elapsed before it was determined that the shot had been fired from a fifth floor window in the Carolina Apartments across the street. By then, the shooter was long gone, having dismantled a high-powered rifle into smaller components, and carried them away in something as innocuous as a gym bag. No one had reported seeing the shooter or witnessing anything suspicious. No doubt the Crime Scene Unit was still at work in the vacant apartment, processing it for forensic evidence.

AS THE HUDSON FAMILY huddled together for comfort and strength, a weary surgeon dressed in green scrubs appeared in the doorway. "Mrs. Hudson?" he asked. Esther Hudson rushed forward to receive word from this saintly being whom she believed her lord had sent especially to save her husband's life.

"We won't know for sure until he awakes, Mrs. Hudson, but I think he's going to be OK. The surgery went smoothly. The bullet grazed the left side of his skull. He's very lucky the bullet did not penetrate his skull, otherwise he would not have made it. And the path the bullet took missed important nerves and arteries. It's a miracle, but I've seen these things happen before. He will have one whopping headache though. And he might experience some short term memory loss."

Esther squeezed her hands together and now the tears rolled down her wrinkled cheeks. "Bless you, sir," she said. "Be all right I give you a hug?"

"Sure," he grinned. "Come on over here."

"See," Lonnie said. "I done told y'all, Mama's never wrong."

Mama Hudson hugged the surgeon in a ferocious bear hug. And the whole huge Hudson clan moved in to claim a part of him. They surrounded the surgeon in one giant embrace so that we couldn't even see the top of his green-capped head. When they parted, Jon settled for shaking the man's hand. I kissed his cheek. Then my tears fell.

"Willie Hudson has worked as our general contractor for the last two years," I told the surgeon with a sob. "He's like family to us."

Briefly his eyes twinkled. "Looks to me like he's got more family than any one man deserves."

Then he shuffled off wearily, dragging his green-bootee feet. How did the man manage to retain a sense of humor, I asked myself. He'd been in surgery for hours. And so had Willie, I reminded myself. Suddenly the whole tragedy which had seemed like a dream, or an episode from *House,* became very, very real.

ON FRIDAY EVENING we met a frantic Melanie at the Brasserie du Soleil. We'd all been absent from our homes for ten days; none of us had any food in our kitchens. We were hungry. And most especially thirsty.

On Saturday, December 22, Melanie and Cameron Jordan, Jon and I, had been married in a double ceremony at St. James Church. Followed by a lavish reception at Melanie and Cam's spectacular historic hunting lodge on the Intracoastal Waterway which, I could proudly claim, Jon and I had restored for them.

Then we'd left for our honeymoons: Jon and I to Pinehurst, Melanie and Cam for a cruise on Cam's yacht, the Hot Momma.

Jon and I had our honeymoon cut short by Willie's shooting. But why was Melanie back home in Wilmington instead off on a cruise with Cam? And where was Cam?

"What happened?" I asked. "Where is Cam? What's going on?"

Jon signaled the bartender and ordered a bottle of wine. Just in time, because I was in need of a very large glass of rich red wine to get my blood flowing. I was starting to shut down.

Before Melanie could reply, the proverbial light bulb went off in my head. You see, Cam absolutely worships the ground Melanie walks on. I've never seen a man so smitten with a woman—well, except for Jon with me. Cam would never have gone off during their honeymoon. There was only one explanation—that is, only one person who could make him do so.

"Nelda!" I exclaimed.

"The Sweetheart of the Silver Screen," Melanie said with rank sarcasm.

Cameron Jordan's mother was a Hollywood legend,

known as the "Sweetheart of the Silver Screen" during the fifties and sixties, when Cam's now deceased father had directed her films. Nelda did not like Melanie. Nelda would not like any woman her only son chose to marry.

"She managed to track us down all the way out in the Atlantic," Melanie explained, "with our cell phones turned off. We wanted peace and quiet, and no intrusions. No crisis calls from his production studio. No deals falling through at my real estate office. But Nelda, being the drama queen that she is, twisted someone's arm until they contacted the Coast Guard to send out a search party for us. And sure enough they found us anchored off the Bimini Islands. Then they delivered the urgent message: Nelda was on her death bed! There was not a second to waste: Cam had to fly to her in New York at once. We had to berth the yacht in Bermuda so that he could fly to New York, and I back here to Wilmington."

"But why didn't you go with him?" Jon asked, then paused to sample the wine. "Fine," he told the bartender perfunctorily, and our glasses were filled.

Melanie took a long swallow before answering. "Because Nelda had her doctor specifically tell Cam that I was not to come. That I would upset her and her condition would worsen. I declare, she must think we're all idiots. How could her condition worsen if she was dying? What's worse than that?"

"Well, what was wrong with her?" Jon asked. "How sick is she? She looked plenty tough to me when I met her at the wedding."

"She is tough. A tough old bird. Tougher than all of us," Melanie said. "She'll outlive all of us. Supposedly she was having a heart attack and called 911. But I know someone who knows someone who practices at Columbia-Presbyterian Hospital so I made inquiries. And she was not having a heart attack. But because of who she is, they are keeping her for observation."

Melanie slammed down her wine glass on the bar with such force, the wine sloshed over the rim and the bartender hurried over with a towel. "Sorry," she said distractedly. "And she has threatened Cam that if he leaves, she'll die."

I shook my head. Poor Melanie. This was not a good way to start a marriage.

"Ashley, Jon, that woman won't rest until she breaks up my marriage. But if she thinks she can do that, she doesn't know who she is up against."

"You're right, Melanie," Jon said. "I think it's safe to say the Hollywood legend has met her match."

THE DINING ROOM AT the Brasserie du Soleil looks out onto the courtyard at Lumina Station where ocean-borne breezes rock empty white rocking chairs on patios, and whirlwinds tease fountain sprays playfully.

Inside, a CD of a chanteuse singing French songs was playing. The room was paneled in dark wood with mirror inserts. The ceiling was bronze pressed tin, the banquettes upholstered in red and gold cut velvet. Our own brasserie was as charming as any I had seen in Paris.

After we brought Melanie up-to-date on Willie's prognosis—that a full recovery was predicted—I said, "Melanie, I definitely think you should fly to New York, check into a very fine hotel so that you have some place nice for you and Cam. That way you can get Cam out of Nelda's apartment and hopefully out from under her thumb. Then you should kill her with kindness while at the same time you convince the doctors to talk sense to Cam."

"I think Ashley's right," Jon said, then turned to our server and ordered the Fettuccini Carbonara.

Melanie, who has guarded her figure a lot longer and with more discipline than I have mine, suggested that she and I share a chicken crepe. "It has mushrooms and goat cheese," she said. "Very tasty so you don't have to eat as much. And the chicken adds protein."

Not eat much? I was all for that. Another secret known to thin women: select very tasty dishes to fool the appetite. And don't forget the protein.

In reply to my suggestion, Melanie said, "As it turns out I can't leave town right now. I've just snared some very, very rich clients."

So what else is new, I thought.

"Speaking of real estate," Jon said to Melanie. "Brian and Jackie Hudson were in Pinehurst. Don't you work with him? We partied with them on New Year's Eve. A fun couple."

And Jackie doesn't care for sweets so that's how she maintains her svelte figure, I recalled. I had just learned two tips from thin women. But how long could I refrain from eating dessert? And how long could I manage with half portions? I didn't know the answer, but I was determined to put myself to the test. My mind wandered, contemplating how my weight-loss plan should consist of kissing Jon every time I got hungry—kiss him until my hunger was replaced by desire. Then forget about food. Hmmmm.

I must have been smiling to myself because Melanie

said, "What's so funny? All I said was that I've got to call Brian as soon as he gets back. Does he know that his uncle has been shot?"

"Yes, we left a message for him at the front desk when we checked out," Jon said. "But there's no love lost between those two branches of the Hudson family. He won't come to the hospital. None of his side will."

"For pity sakes," she cried. "Perhaps we should count our blessings that we don't come from one of those enormous families where everybody is feuding with everyone else. Now as I was saying, I met a very rich couple in Bimini who are pining away for a Southern mansion. Chinese. They are Chinese. I think they watched *Gone With the Wind* one too many times. They have this notion that a large, white, columned mansion will somehow transform them into Americans."

"Well, why not buy up our Southern mansions?" Jon's voice dripped with sarcasm. "They already own our national debt. What's a Southern mansion or two?"

Melanie eyed him suspiciously but did not respond. He'd better not rain on her parade, her look said. "Actually, I think they're already in town. They were sailing for Wilmington when Cam and I met them. They'll be docked out at the Wrightsville Marina for the rest of the winter. Oh, Ashley, Jon, wait until you see their yacht. It is unbelievable. Incredible. And we're all invited aboard on Saturday night for an early Chinese New Year's party. In their culture they start celebrating early."

Jon and I exchanged glances. A party we'd try to get out of, sure enough. Jon did not like parties thrown by strangers. Neither did I.

Melanie continued, "I'm determined to find them the

mansion of their dreams, and see to it that they spend a bundle for it. That's why I have to call Brian. I'll need his help with the legalities of selling to foreigners. Exchange rates. Chinese banks. All that legal stuff."

She grimaced. "I'll do anything to survive this dreadful real estate market. The depreciation is killing homeowners. Everyone is too afraid to sell, and everyone is too afraid to buy. So I've got to get the Chengs' business."

She brightened. "I know what I'll do, I'll buy them the most fabulous gift. That will make them beholden to me so they won't go with anyone else, like Faye Brock who is just the sweetest thing and everyone loves her."

I reached across the table and patted her hand. She was hurting. The market was a dismal mess. "Everyone loves you, too, Melanie. Jon and I will do what we can to help. Won't we Jon?"

He gave me a startled look, appalled. Was I dragging him to the party after all?

"I'll help you find the perfect gift. And I know just the place. The Crescent Moon gift shop has the most fabulous glass art objects. Hand made. We don't want you giving her that crappy 'made in China' stuff."

I snickered at my own joke.

THREE

ON A SEASONABLY CHILLY Saturday morning with temperatures in the high forties, Jon and I pulled into Nun Street. The back of his Escalade was loaded with groceries from our run out to the Fresh Market at Mayfaire. The North Carolina based store offered many prepared foods for people like Jon and me who do not cook and who were helpless in the kitchen.

"As much as I love this car," he said for the umpteenth time, "it's a gas guzzler and we've got to trade it in for something green."

"We'll take a loss," I responded again. Actually I felt sentimental about Jon's Escalade. How many job sites had we traveled to in it? He'd picked me up for our first date in this car.

"Can't be helped," he replied.

"Soon," I said, as I had been saying.

Nun Street was quiet, as if the whole street was sleeping in after one too many New Year's festivities. The Verandas Bed & Breakfast down the street was atypically silent. The innkeepers, our friends Chuck and Dennis, vacationed at this time of year, traveling to exotic locales, such as India and Nepal.

The only noise on our street came from the parade of placards that marched along in front yards, shouting: "PROTECT OUR AIR—WATER—CHILDREN stoptitan.org." Luring Titan Cement into the county was the ill-conceived brainchild of some misguided county commissioners. But the mercury and hydrochloric acid that the manufacture of cement would discharge into our atmosphere and ground water—not to mention other cancer-causing toxins—was simply too harmful a tradeoff for a few, low-paying jobs. The guilty county commissioners had been voted out of office, but the battle raged on. Don't they always?

"Oh, no!" I exclaimed as we pulled up to my house and I caught sight of the two gun-toting villains on my front porch. "It's Nick…"

"And her," Jon finished.

There, pacing impatiently on the porch of my 1860 Queen Anne house, was my former husband, Homicide Detective Nicholas Yost. And his untrustworthy sidekick, Detective Diane Sherwood. Diane had the hots for Nick. For years she had blamed me for standing in her way. What's your excuse now, Diane? Duh. Unless, of course, she had landed him.

"Just when you think things can't get any worse, those two show up," I complained to Jon, and we braced ourselves as we got out of the car.

"Leave the groceries. I'm not inviting the demonic duo into our house," Jon muttered.

Despite the irritation their presence provoked, I burst out laughing. And stopped to smile up at Jon. "Demonic duo, huh? Wish I'd said that." My hero. I took his hand as we crossed the sidewalk.

"Hi Nick. Diane," I said in a voice that was intended to sound as chilly as the temperature.

As we mounted the steps to the porch, Jon asked, "What can we do for you, Nick?"

"Ashley. Jon," Nick said. He didn't offer to shake hands. Fine with me.

Sherwood nodded, then flipped her heavy, shoulder length chestnut hair. She had on dark glasses, small lenses without frames. In all fairness, she was a pretty woman who worked out religiously. No muffin tops for Detective Sherwood. Self-consciously, I pulled my jacket closer around my middle.

"We want to ask you some questions about the shooting on New Year's Day. The attempted murder of Willie Hudson," Sherwood said. "Can we go inside?"

Jon crossed his arms on his chest and planted his feet firmly on the porch floor. "This is not a convenient time," he said, yet managing admirably to sound pleasant.

"We can't tell you anything anyway," I said with far less tact. "We weren't even here, as I'm sure you know."

I linked my arm through Jon's. "We were on our honeymoon in Pinehurst." Now my voice was very pleasant, almost purring, just the attitude I wished to convey.

Nick cleared his throat. I couldn't see his eyes. He was wearing shades, too. But I knew from hours of gazing into them that they were a beautiful hazel. They used to smolder with passion; passion for me. Now I hoped they were smoldering with resentment—and jealousy. Can't help it. I'm only human.

The man was hot, there was no denying that. He was lean waisted and broad shouldered, with crisp light brown hair. A beautifully shaped face. But whatever love I had felt for him, whatever passion once burned within me for him, was definitely a thing of the past.

Dead and buried. The flames doused. In all truthfulness, he had killed the tender feelings I once felt for him. And my love for Jon had buried them. Finished. Finito.

"We tried to talk to Hudson this morning," Nick said. "But he's on pain meds plus experiencing short-term memory loss. He doesn't remember why he was in the observatory at the Bellamy Mansion or even that he was there."

"Did you talk to his family?" Jon asked.

"Yes. And they said he was working on a job for you two," Nick replied.

Jon moved closer to me and wrapped an arm around my waist protectively. "That's correct," he said, again managing to remain agreeable and cooperative. "Our firm has volunteered to restore the mansion's belvedere. Willie was getting a jump start on evaluating what has to be done. Now we're all taking some time off to show our respect for him and his family."

Nick pulled off his sunglasses, looked from Jon to me with a frown. When Nick smiles, he has adorable dimples in his cheeks. But Nick rarely smiles. That, in itself, should have been a warning sign that he was not the man for me. I love to laugh.

"We want to know what he was doing up there. And more importantly, we want to know who knew he'd be there at that hour. Eight o'clock on New Year's Day isn't your usual time for a contractor to be on a job."

I wrapped my arm around Jon's waist, feeling the tension this hostile cross examination was causing both of us, on top of Willie's near death. "Willie was up in the belvedere because we are going to be restoring the windows there," I said evenly. "And any number of people could have known that he'd be there. It wasn't a secret that we had volunteered to do the job. There was an item in the *Star-News*. And an announcement in Preservation North Carolina's newsletter. Most everyone in the historic district knew."

"And why that hour and that day?" Jon interjected defensively. "Because, as you well know, the mansion is a museum, open to the public, and we have to work around the hours and days they are open. Until recently, the belvedere was on the tour."

"Did Hudson have any enemies?" Sherwood asked.

"No," Jon said emphatically. "Willie Hudson is a respected leader in his church and in the African-American community. Everyone thought the world of him."

"Obviously, not everyone," Nick said.

Jon and I said nothing.

"The bullet could have been intended for one of his crew," Sherwood speculated.

"Who was working with him?" I asked. In all the excitement and worry I had never thought to ask that question.

Nick pulled out a small notebook and searched the pages. "Dwayne Hudson and Lonnie Hudson were scheduled to meet him, but he was alone when shot. The others found him when they arrived minutes later."

"Oh," I said. "Lonnie is his son."

"And Dwayne is his grandson, son of Willie's son Mason," Jon added. "What a shock for them."

"We know about the intricate family relationships," Sherwood said testily.

Honestly, I wanted to slap that woman so badly my palm itched and I took a second to scratch it.

"Those two got any enemies?" Nick asked.

"I wouldn't know," Jon answered, taking a step toward our front door, keys in his outstretched hand.

"You tell us something," I said. "Whose apartment was the shot fired from?"

"No tenant," Nick replied. "Up for rent. Unoccupied."

"Well, who had the keys?" I asked the obvious.

Diane Sherwood got all huffy. "You know we can't discuss an ongoing investigation with you."

But Nick ignored her. After all, we had been husband and wife. I assumed he still trusted me. "The front desk had the keys. But when we got there the door to the apartment was unlocked. The desk clerk admits the painting crew could have left the door unlocked for the carpet people."

"Paint crew? Meaning all the surfaces were newly painted," I said. "And that means that any fingerprints you found were either those of the painters or the shooter."

Diane Sherwood gave me a withering look. Diane likes to pretend that I am dumb.

"I hope the apartment's management and the PD are taking measures to secure the place," I said.

"Don't worry about what the PD is doing," Diane said.

"Of course, we're taking measures," Nick said. "We've got a large uniform presence in the area, very

visible, at the apartments and around the Bellamy
Mansion. The Carolina Apartments has been secured,
the doors to vacant apartments locked, a security officer in the lobby. A forensic team is out, too. We still
have not found the spent bullet."

"Don't you think the chief knows how important
tourism is to this town?" Diane asked.

Jon had had enough. "OK. That's enough. We've
got ice cream melting in the car and groceries to
unload."

"How domestic," Sherwood commented under her
breath but I heard her.

I wanted to shout: Scoot. Scram. Like I did to the
squirrel that invaded our birdfeeder.

My good friend Kiki would have said: Be gone or
I'll put a curse on you and turn you into a toad. But
then Kiki is a witch. And I am not. If only.

"DO WE REALLY HAVE to go to that party?" Jon asked,
after we had put away the groceries and were settled at
the kitchen table with Swiss cheese and turkey Panini
sandwiches and iced tea.

"Oh, sweetie, I'm so sorry. I promised Melanie. You
could see how discouraged she was."

"But what good will it do her for us to be there?"

"Just moral support, darling. She likes having us in
her corner. Melanie is not nearly as confident as she
puts on."

He leaned across the table and kissed the tip of my
nose. "You're a softie, you know that? OK, except for
my Granny Campbell and your Aunt Ruby and Binkie,
Melanie and Cam are our only family. And we do have
to take care of family."

"I love you for that," I said, and checked the wall clock. "Visiting hours at the medical center start soon. I hope Willie is awake. And that he knows us."

FOUR

THE SURGEON WAS LEAVING Willie's room as we entered. He was dressed in a suit and tie, and did not look anywhere near as weary as he had the day of the surgery. He seemed to recognize Jon and me because he said, "He's coming along nicely." He glanced across the room to Esther Hudson. "Mrs. Hudson is right. Sometimes miracles do happen. And I need all the help I can get, so I'm very grateful for this one."

Esther Hudson gave him a big smile, then welcomed us with, "Come on in, y'all. Don't be shy." Jon and I approached Willie's bed hesitantly. His head was swathed in bandages. And there were cuts on his face and arms from the flying glass. For someone who had just had head surgery on Thursday, he was remarkably alert.

"Hey, big guy," Jon said with a cheerfulness he could not possibly feel.

Willie is anything but big. He is in his seventies, small and wizened, and in the hospital bed he looked even smaller and very frail.

"Hey there, Ashley. Jon," Willie said. "They're telling me I'm a wonder. Gonna be the poster boy for head injuries."

"Oh Willie, you remember us," I murmured, taking his hand in my own. "We are so sorry this happened to you. We don't understand anything that has happened. Why would someone shot you?"

"Did you see anything?" Jon asked. "Anything at all?"

"I still don't have my memory back 'bout being up there in that belvedere. Last thing I recall was eating Esther's delicious hot cakes for breakfast that morning. After that, nothing. Till I woke up here this morning. Your ex was here, Ashley, with that woman detective, asking all kinds of questions."

Esther harrumphed. "Wanted to know if we had enemies. What kind of question is that? He doesn't have an enemy in the world and neither do I. We spend our days helping folks, not making enemies of them."

Willie said, "I'm getting too old for this, Jon. Too old to be climbing round up there in that belvedere. It's time for me to retire, to turn the business over to the youngsters. I'm thinking on that."

"Oh Willie," I cried again. "What would we do without you? You've got more knowledge about how these old houses in Wilmington were constructed than anyone."

"But we can understand you might feel that way, Willie," Jon said. "After the traumatic experience you've had you must be re-evaluating everything. But this isn't the time to make a big decision. Why don't you wait until you're feeling like your old self again?"

"Whatever you decide, we'll respect your decision," I said. "You know there's a strong police presence around the mansion now, ensuring our safety whenever we go back up into the belvedere."

"He is not retiring," Esther said firmly. "Do you know that folks who retire live, on average, two years? I don't want that happening to my husband. Besides," she said, turning to Willie, "you'd be underfoot. Won't know what to do with yourself. No sir, as long as you are healthy, you stick to your profession. Cut your hours if you want, but you are not hanging around the house."

Casting her warm brown eyes my way, she said, "You know what women say, don't you, Ashley? 'Marry for life, but not for lunch.'" She grinned.

Willie glanced at Esther, then back to us. "We'll talk 'bout this later when I've got my strength and my memory back. Been lying here thinking about the old days, 'bout my daddy and his daddy before him. There's something 'bout getting old that makes you feel closer to the ones that came before you. Don't know if I ever told you this but it was my great-granddaddy who installed all that fancy plumbing and the gas lines in the Bellamy house.

"Not mansion, mind you, but house. That's what the Bellamy family used to call it: house."

"I had no idea your family were the original plumbers," I said. "The plumbing was extraordinary for its day. So far ahead of its time. Imagine, it was eighteen-sixty and they had hot and cold running water, and warm showers. That was just about unheard of."

"And it was your family who were the plumbers?" Jon asked with awe.

"Yes sir. My great-granddaddy Wilfred Hudson. I was named for him. He was a freedman. One of the finest craftsmen Wilmington has ever known. An educated man, too. He was taught to read and write at James Sampson's School for Free Negroes. Then he taught his sons to read."

"And his daughters," Esther interjected.

"You know the Bellamy Mansion was built by African-American craftsmen and artisans."

"We did know that," I said.

"There were many whites in those days who resented that, too," Esther said. "But they didn't get the jobs because they weren't as talented as our people were. But they were quite vocal 'bout their grievances. One of the town leaders said he didn't want any more animosity between the races than we already had, and he put a stop to it."

"I see a lot of my father in Lonnie. And Lonnie would like to take over the business," Willie said. "He's a good boy, a hard worker."

"And smart," Esther said. "You can give him a bigger role. I've got no problem with that."

Lonnie was at least fifty-five, hardly a boy, but I suppose you are always a boy or a girl to your parents.

"Now Mason's got it in his head that he's gonna get taken on at the new state port they're fixin' to build down at Southport. Says there's gonna be lotsa money to be made on that project."

"The last I heard," Jon said, "they haven't even come up with funds for the reconnaissance study yet."

AT FOUR THAT AFTERNOON I met Melanie at the Crescent Moon gift shop in the Cotton Exchange down by the river. My sister Melanie is a heart stopper with her long flowing auburn hair, big green eyes, and ivory complexion. At twenty-one she had been voted Miss North Carolina, representing our state in the Miss America beauty pageant. She hasn't changed much since then, still has her killer figure, and knows how to dress.

She has had more boyfriends that I can count. Many of them were bad boys. And then darling Cameron Jordan came to town, cast one look in her direction, and fell really hard. It took Melanie a couple of years and a few disastrous experiences for the bad boys' appeal to wear thin, and for her to finally appreciate what a prince she had in Cameron Jordan.

Melanie and I do not look anything alike. I look like Daddy, the late Superior Court Judge Peter Wilkes, with his dark hair, gray eyes, and serious expression.

Melanie is the spitting image of Mama, Claire Chastain Wilkes, of the Savannah Chastains.

Mama and Daddy reside in heaven now, having left us girls behind to look after each other. Thank god, I had Cameron to help me manage Melanie. She can be rather a handful—unpredictable and headstrong.

Today she had on a little dress with a matching coat, in a carmely brown tone. While I, not having much time to dress that morning, had thrown on a hoodie and sweat pants. But at least in a sweet pink that complimented my skin tones.

The gift shop was filled with light from two large windows, and the glass shelves were backlit so that everything seemed to sparkle and shimmer. As we strolled around the shop, admiring displays of hand-blown glass art objects, she said, "You look good with long hair, Shug. Didn't I tell you that length would help straighten out the curl? You have just enough natural wave and curl for it to look pretty."

I grinned. I was feeling on top of the world after my visit with Willie and knowing he was going to make it. "Yes, big sister, you are always right."

She examined me closely. "I declare, Ashley, you

are positively radiant. There is not a skin care product in this world that can give you that glow. That glow comes from getting good sex, and lots of it."

"Melanie!" I exclaimed, glancing around to see if the other customer in the store had heard her.

"Don't 'Melanie' me. I've had enough good sex in my life to recognize the result." Then she pouted and gave me a look of utter chagrin. "Just wish I was getting some now. Here it is supposed to be my honeymoon, and what am I doing? Sleeping alone. A pox on that Nelda Cameron!"

The other customer left the shop and Joan and Mike Loch, the owners, hurried up to greet us. "Melanie Wilkes! And Ashley. How are you girls?" Joan said. "Only you've got new last names now. I'll have to remember."

"That's all right, Joan," I said. "Both Melanie and I are keeping our surnames. Wilkes we were born and Wilkes we shall remain."

"Sure enough," Joan said. "Times have changed."

"Are you guys still living on the river?" Melanie asked.

Joan and Mike, a glass blower himself, live on a boat, a forty-two foot Jefferson Sundeck, docked near the Port of Wilmington.

"Because if you ever decide you want more space and a backyard, it is a buyer's market out there. You can practically steal a house."

"Melanie," Joan said sweetly, "I promise you if Mike and I find time away from this shop to go house hunting, it will definitely be with you. Now what can I do for you? Are you looking for something special?"

"Very special," Melanie replied. "I want the most

impressive piece of glass art you've got in the shop. It's for a very important client."

"Well, then," Mike told us, "you are standing right in front of the best. These are the works of our premier artist Rick Satava. Aren't they phenomenal? They are glass jellyfish. Rick uses ancient techniques to create original designs in handblown glass."

"The colors are so vivid," Melanie commented.

"I like this one," I said, indicating a blue glass "jelly" that glowed almost lifelike inside a clear glass globe.

"That one is called Blue Moon," Joan said. "People who enter the shop immediately gravitate to Satava's work. And the Blue Moon is most popular because of its gorgeous blue glow."

"Did you know that jellyfish have been found on earth for over six hundred and fifty million years—before sharks and even dinosaurs?" Mike said. "They have no head, heart, brain, bones, cartilage or real eyes. Yet they're among the major predators in the ocean. Their tentacles carry stinging cells that are among the most complicated found anywhere in the animal kingdom."

Melanie laughed. "Sounds like some men I've known. No brains, no backbones, just stinging tentacles."

The Lochs just smiled at her politely. How could they know that her husband had flown off in the middle of their honeymoon to attend the supposed "death bed" of his manipulative mother?

"How much is the Blue Moon?" Melanie asked.

"The Blue Moon is one thousand fifty dollars," Joan said.

"I'll take it. Can you gift wrap it very special? I want to impress someone."

"The Blue Moon will definitely impress your client," Joan assured us, and removed the glass globe from the display case to take around the counter to wrap while Mike wrote up the sale.

"Melanie, that is some extravagant gift," I said. "And you know how fickle your clients can be. There's no assurance this couple will buy from …"

"Melanie!" a woman screeched from the open door.

I turned to see a petite woman with shiny blue-black hair. She had large dark eyes and was dressed in tights with one of those bulky knit tunic sweaters that were so popular this winter but that Melanie assured me would quickly go out of style. They were so unflattering.

"Candi!" Melanie greeted. "What a surprise to see you here, sweetie. I thought you'd be preparing for the party."

The Chinese woman approached us with a large, pleased-with-herself-smile plastered on her face. She waved a hand, indifferent. "Oh, I've got a party planner to handle all that for me."

Her speech was rapid-fire, high-pitched, choppy, and as irritating as nails on a chalkboard.

"Candi, this is my sister Ashley. Ashley, this is my new client Candi Cheng."

Candi's hand was birdlike in mine as we shook hands. "I'm pleased to meet you, Candi."

Candi flicked me over with a cool glance, made a quick decision that I was unimportant, then fixed Melanie with the most intense stare. In fact, I could see immediately, this woman was very, very intense. She vibrated almost as eerily as the glass jellyfish.

"Melanie! Your office told me I could find you here. I had to come right away. I have found it!"

Melanie just looked at her, unblinking, uncomprehending.

"The house!" Candi shrieked. "I have found the house. I must have it. A glorious white mansion up on the hill." She waved a child-size arm. "Enormous white two-story columns! There is even a fountain in the roundabout out front."

I knew exactly which house she was referring to. Intelligence shot across Melanie's face as she got it, too.

"It's called bell something," Candi shrieked. "The bell something mansion."

"MELANIE!" I SHRIEKED almost as piercingly as Candi had. "The Bellamy Mansion is not for sale. What is it with you and your crazy clients? Only recently you represented those dreadful Pogues who insisted they were going to buy Captain Pettigrew's house even though it was not for sale."

Candi had breezed out of the Crescent Moon, as airily as she had breezed in. Melanie had collected the beautifully wrapped Blue Moon glass "jelly," and together we'd tramped down the wooden staircase and out into the parking lot of the Cotton Exchange. I had been berating Melanie as she'd stomped on ahead of me to her car. I trailed along behind, complaining bitterly, "She cannot buy the Bellamy Mansion!"

Melanie turned abruptly. "I know that. I know that it is a stewardship property of Preservation North Carolina and not for sale. I'll just have to find her something similar now that I know what she likes."

Melanie and her clients can be so infuriating.

A cab entered the parking lot and pulled up along side us where we stood arguing next to Melanie's bright red Mercedes CLK 500 Cabriolet convertible.

The rear window of the cab slid down. A man's voice called, "You babes need a lift?"

Melanie took one look, jumped off the ground in a twirl reminiscent of her high school cheerleading days, and squealed, "Cam!"

In an instant he bounded out of the cab and wrapped her in his arms. "You're home!" she cried.

FIVE

ON SATURDAY EVENING we boarded a launch at the Wrightsville Marina to sail out to Candi and Han's spectacular yacht, *The Glowing,* so named because the Chinese translation of Candi was "glowing." Their luxury yacht had created quite a buzz of excitement among yachting enthusiasts in the area. Not since the days of the Pembroke Joneses had Wilmington seen any ship as lavish as the Chengs'. At one hundred feet in length, it featured a sport deck, a media lounge, an open air champagne bar, an immense salon, and state rooms for twelve.

The weather was nippy and I huddled in my coat and in Jon's arms for warmth as we crossed the darkened waterway toward the brilliantly lit yacht with its mega watt illumination lighting up the night. The Intracoastal Waterway is eerily pitch black at night. I'd pinned up my hair with jeweled combs so I didn't have to worry about the damp wind turning it into a frizzy mess.

We reached the yacht and a crew member assisted us up the ramp. Melanie first, then me, Cam, and lastly Jon. He was dressed in a beautifully-cut midnight blue suit that showed off his golden blonde good looks. I had on a black silk cocktail dress.

Inside the salon, Melanie slipped off her coat and handed it to a waiting attendant, and it was clear to me that she would be the most dazzling woman at the party.

Her gown was a pale peach, embroidered with sequins, and fit like a second skin. Melanie did not jog, nor do Pilates, or work out at a gym, so how did she maintain that gorgeous figure? Beats me.

Cam was immediately at her side with an arm flung possessively around her waist. She's my wife, his devotion shouted, and you other guys, back off!

A tiny, red-haired woman bore down on us as relentlessly as a Coast Guard cutter after a pirate ship. "Melanie!" she screeched. I'd recognize that irritating high-pitched squeal anywhere. Our hostess, Candi. But what had she done to her hair?

"Melanie, darling," she trilled in her sing-song voice, and kissed the air at Melanie's cheek. Was this air kissing also a Chinese custom? Or had Candi been watching the remake of Anita Loos's Thirties classic, *The Women?* There had been a lot of air kissing in that revival.

Melanie zoomed in on Candi's new hair color with the ferocity of a feral cat on a dozing mouse. The frosty gleam in her eye said she abhorred Candi's new red hair which was an exact match for Melanie's own natural color.

"You've changed your hair," Melanie said with a forced smile.

"Oh, do you like it?" Candi asked and patted the perm that had produced waves and curls just like Melanie's. "I've always wanted to be a redhead. The hairstylist you recommended was fab. She knew just how to do my hair when I described the style I had in mind."

"Melanie is going to snatch that hair stylist bald," Jon whispered to me.

"Don't say a word," I warned him.

Jon and Cam continued to stare. "I'm not sure ..." Cam started to say.

But Melanie had not risen to the status of billion-dollar producer by insulting her clients. Her smile broadened and her tone became as syrupy as a bottle of Aunt Jemima's own when she said, "You look gorgeous, Candi. The style and color suit you."

"Oh, do you really think so, Melanie? Because your opinion is most critical to me. These other women," and her shallow arm rake indicated the bevy of well-turned out women who were her guests, "what do they know about style?"

Only those who know Melanie as well as Jon, Cam, and I could spot her fake smile—a smile that had been practiced endlessly in front of a mirror during her pageant days. Or detect that the syrup in her voice would soon harden to rock. Oh, Candi would pay dearly for this lapse in judgment, and she would pay big, in big bucks.

"Come on, Melanie," Candi whined, catching Melanie's hand. "I want you to meet some very important people."

But Melanie withdrew her hand and said, "Show us to the powder room first, Candi. I'm a little windblown."

And as Candi motioned to an attendant who scurried forward rapidly, Melanie grabbed my arm. "Come on, Shug, let's go comb our hair."

Candi instructed the attendant to show us to the day head, then without so much as a greeting to me, or a glance at Jon and Cam, she turned on her heel to mingle with other, more important guests than we.

INSIDE THE DAY HEAD, it was my turn to screech. "Oh my god, Melanie," I cried, as I ran my hand over the smooth cream-colored lavatory basin and counter top.

"What?" Melanie asked distractedly, gazing at herself in the mirror, and plumping up her waves and curls. "Now I'll have to get a new do," she groaned. "The nerve of that skinny-assed skank."

"Oh, Melanie, forget it. She looks ridiculous. Anyone can see how silly she is. Do you know what this is?" I asked with alarm, my palm caressing the sink bowl, my voice as high-pitched as Candi's.

"Wait till I get my hands around the neck of that hair stylist," Melanie threatened. "How dare she duplicate my style and color on that…pompous creature?"

"Melanie," I cried, "forget the hair. This is ivory! Ivory! They've made a sink bowl out of ivory. Now we know why this yacht was built in Hong Kong. There's no American company that would commit such a sin. Why there are laws against the importing and sale of ivory."

"What?" Melanie said, still fingering her hair with a repulsed expression on her face.

"Ivory, Melanie. Ivory. Forget your hair. Some poacher shot an elephant just so that…what did you call her?…that skinny-assed skank? She does have the figure of a pre-pubescent eleven year old, doesn't she? Anyway, listen to me. Those elephants suffer. They are left to bleed to death after the poachers hack off their tusks."

Melanie stared at me, an expression of horror on her face.

"Oh, Melanie, dump that dreadful woman. You don't

need her. You're the best realtor in this town. Everyone knows that."

Melanie redirected her focus to the sink bowl. "Are you sure it's ivory? Maybe it's something else. Corian?"

"No, it's ivory all right."

"I saw a show on the Nature Channel about how the poachers bring down elephants. I detest anyone who is cruel to animals or who profits from the cruelty. And also those who support those miserable…miserable… If that selfish bitch has outfitted her yacht with illegal exotic materials, well, I'm going to stick it to her good. She is going to pay, and pay big time. I'm going to make her suffer just like that elephant suffered."

"What do you have in mind?" I asked.

"I haven't figured that out yet. But it is going to be good, and I'm going to make the biggest sale this town has ever witnessed."

As we left the day head we found Jackie Hudson waiting for us. Jackie was impatient. And livid. Practically stamping her high-heeled sandaled foot. "Did you see it?" she screeched. "They are in every head on this ship! Elephant tusks! Elephant tusks used for sink basins and countertops. Turns my stomach!"

"Yes, we saw," I said glumly.

"Come with me," Jackie said. "Let me show you something." And she led us down a hallway and into the library. "Do you see this paneling? Han has been showing it off to the guests. Brazilian bigleaf mahogany. Can you believe it? That fool is destroying the rain forest so he can panel a room and boast about it to others who are just as easily impressed and ignorant as he."

"Oh my gosh, Jackie," I said, "you're right. I am

offended. Really offended. I'm going to find Jon and we are leaving this party right now. I know Jon feels the same way we do."

"Wait a moment, Shug," Melanie called. "You can't leave without Cam and me, and I've got to stay here and reel in my fish."

I turned to her. "Melanie, she is so besotted with you, you have nothing to worry about. The next thing we know, she'll be trying to borrow your clothes."

"I don't think you two are taking this sacrilege very seriously," Jackie said with hostility.

"We do take it seriously," I tried to reassure her.

Jackie fumed, "It's a crime, what they have done. Here I've been leading the campaign against Titan Cement so that we can preserve our air quality, and those two leave behind their polluted cities and sail into our port with a boat load of contraband. Well, I won't stand for it. I am going to expose them. I am going to get even with them if it means I have to personally throw them overboard and sink this befouled ship myself!"

SIX

OUT IN THE SALON, the party was in full swing with servers offering trays of hors d'oeuvres and flutes of champagne. Melanie allowed herself to be dragged off by Candi. I could see the wheels spinning in Melanie's brain as she narrowed her eyes into dangerous slits while scheming about how she was going to get her hands on Candi's money.

I FOUND JON AND CAM in a smoking lounge off the main salon, cigars in hand, and deep in discussion with Brian Hudson and Han Cheng about something that had captured their total interest. Jackie Hudson was now out on the dance floor, fox-trotting with one of those heavy-set men who turn out to be incredibly light on their feet when dancing. She was giving him an earful, and I recognized him as an environmental attorney who was associated with the future international container terminal. How many elephants had been slaughtered to outfit this yacht, I wondered. And would Jackie's dance partner be as outraged as she?

I slipped in between Jon and Cam. Jon touched me lightly on the back, then turned to refocus on what Brian was saying. I was still stewing over the poached ivory and barely listened until I realized Brian was again discussing the bail-out and how it might impact on his intention to collect outstanding debts.

"As you know, the government is funding this huge bail-out of our financial institutions," Brian was saying. "Citigroup is receiving three hundred billion. One of the stipulations is that they clean up their books. By that I mean they must collect on notes they've been carrying on the books for decades. Simply forgotten. Overlooked."

"How is your firm involved?" Cam asked. Cameron Jordan is a television and motion picture industry leader, and there is little about the current economic situation that he is not aware of. "I've got to admit, I'm not too sure I approve of these bailouts."

"But your government has got to do something," Han interjected. "Your financial institutions with their sale of credit default swaps, which smacks more of Los Vegas than Wall Street, and their fraudulent accounting practices have brought down the entire global economy. My country continues to pour our revenues into yours. Our exports have fallen. The losses I have personally suffered…Now there may be a substantial delay in the building of the new port. And where is my container fleet to deliver our goods?"

Brian explained, "Citigroup has been downsizing. Laying off employees right and left in an effort to improve their bottom line and avoid bankruptcy. So they have contracted out a lot of the work involved with this bailout. And they've selected our firm to handle the New Hanover County area. They've turned over the documents to us and we get paid when we collect. Once they prove they are cleaning up old loans, they get a bigger piece of the taxpayers' pie."

"And you're going to collect the old outstanding debts from our area?" I asked.

"Correct, Ashley. And as we discussed on New Year's Eve, it is surprising who some of the debtors turn out to be. As I told you, the Bellamy Mansion is one of the debtors on Citigroup's books. Some old notes that got transferred over during bank mergers, and well, just got overlooked and were basically ignored."

"Until now?" Jon said as disbelieving as I that this could be happening.

Brian nodded his head up and down. "Surprised the hell out of me, too. Come on, y'all, let's sit down and I'll explain exactly how this operation is going to work."

We moved over to the banquettes along the wall and Brian began his lengthy tale.

"I expect y'all know the history of the mansion. Except for you, Han," Brian said.

Han grinned. "I've been getting an earful from Candi about that mansion. She has her heart set on owning it." He chuckled lightly.

Jon and I made eye contact and shared a silent vow: Over our dead bodies.

"Of course we know the history of the mansion," I said.

"OK, I'll try not to be redundant then," Brian continued. "When the mansion was under construction, Dr. Bellamy practiced competitive shopping for the materials needed. So, even though there was an ongoing political conflict with the Northern states over the issue of slavery prior to the war, Dr. Bellamy purchased much of the materials and fixtures for the house from New York and Philadelphia where he could get the best products at the best prices.

"He and the architects used a purchasing agent out of New York, name of Thaddeus Greensleeves.

Greensleeves would receive the drawings and speci-
fications from the architect, Rufus Bunnell, and then
he would shop the manufacturers in New York City,
Brooklyn, and Philadelphia until he found just what
the architects had in mind. Greensleeves then would arrange for the transport of the materials by train or ship,
and handle the paperwork. All for a fee, of course."

"I never heard about anyone named Greensleeves
involved in the construction of the Bellamy Mansion," I said, "and I have researched the building of
the mansion."

"I don't want to get into a dispute about this matter
with local historians," Brian said dismissively. "All
I know is I've got the documentation to prove my
case."

"You've got the original documents?" I asked.

"Of course. Citigroup turned them over to my firm,"
Brian replied.

He paused to relight his cigar which had burnt out.

"Because I'd like to take a look at them," I said.

"Well, I don't know, Ashley. You are not a party to
this case. Look, let me explain. When the Civil War
started, the Confederacy put into effect a policy called
'condemnation.' All debts owed to Northern merchants
had to be paid to the Confederate government. Thus,
Dr. Bellamy paid the Confederacy for outstanding debts
on items like a dozen elaborate gasoliers, shutters for
all the windows, all of the hardware, brass cornices,
art objects, carpets, antiques, marble, mahogany, burled
walnut. The list goes on and on. As the war waged on
longer than expected and Northern tradesmen like Jenkins and Porter grew anxious and gave up hope of ever
being paid, Greensleeves arranged for a bank called

the East River Bank & Trust to buy the outstanding notes at a discount. Later, East River was bought out by Bowery Savings, then Bowery Savings was bought by a Los Angeles bank.

"Long story short, through a series of acquisitions, Citigroup ended up owning the assets and liabilities from the original East River Bank. And among those assets are notes owed by Dr. Bellamy."

"How much money are we talking about here?" Cam asked with a frown.

Brian arched curly eyebrows. "With one hundred and fifty years of compounded interest on the original debt, plus penalties and legal fees, we're talking almost seventy-five thousand dollars."

"Whoa!" I cried. "Have you thought this through, Brian? The mansion is a stewardship property of Preservation NC. They'd never be able to come up with seventy-five thousand dollars to settle an old debt!"

"They would not," Jon echoed. "Why, it's taken them years to raise the money for renovations. There's no extra cash lying around. And now, with times hard on everyone, donations are down."

"And," Cam added, "state revenues have fallen as well so we can't go running to the state legislature for an appropriation."

Han had been studying Brian intently. Now, with his hand cupping his chin, he said thoughtfully, "Do I understand you correctly, Brian? If the original note is not paid, Citigroup would have the option to foreclose on the property? To force its sale?"

Brian replied evenly, "It is conceivable that is what could happen. Of course, we would negotiate, do everything we could to prevent such a thing from happening, that is foreclosure. But, yes, the teeth in the bite of collection is foreclosure. We could force the sale."

"Well," Han said slowly, as if thinking out loud, "what if an interested party made an offer to Preservation NC that they could not refuse? This interested party would pay the old debt and its interest and penalties, and in addition, offer a most attractive, above-market price for the mansion. Would they not be willing to sell under those circumstances?"

All eyes turned to Brian.

"By interested party, I assume you are referring to yourself and Candi," Brian replied. "What sort of figure did you have in mind?"

"Naturally, I must consult with my financial advisers," Han, ever cautious, said, "but Candi has her heart set on that mansion. And she has found a local, established realtor to handle the sale."

He turned to me. "Melanie Wilkes. Your sister."

"And my wife," Cam said, and seemed not at all pleased to have Melanie dragged into this discussion.

Then Han went on, "So the way I see it, we will have the mansion appraised by an independent appraiser. Then we'll add a hefty amount on top of the appraisal, settle the old debt, and proceed to closing."

"Oh, I don't…" I started to say.

"They'd never…" Jon started to say.

Brian interrupted, "But Jon, Ashley, isn't that precisely the mission of Preservation NC? They sell historic properties to individuals who will restore and maintain them. They should have no problem with this transaction. And as I see it, doubtless they'd have no choice. If, as you say, they cannot come up with seventy-five thousand dollars to pay the old debt, they'd have no choice but to sell. This would be a way out for them."

"No choice," Han said as if the matter was settled. "I can't wait to tell Candi."

SEVEN

"IF THAT WASN'T the party from hell, I don't know what was," I told Jon as we got into the Escalade. Then we followed Melanie and Cam across the bridge and made a quick left onto Airlie Road. After a quarter mile, we whipped into their tree-lined driveway that snaked out to the Intracoastal Waterway and the lodge. Jon and I had completed restoration of the lodge in late December, in time for us to hold our wedding reception there.

We left our coats in the reception hall and moved into the library that had been modeled after the library at the Biltmore House. Last year, Melanie and I had made several trips to America's Castle in Asheville to get ideas and inspiration from George Vanderbilt's mansion. The solid, built-in bookcases were made of oak, stained to resemble mahogany. And there were rows of books, many on the theatre and the movie industry from Cam's collection that he had brought to their marriage. The older volumes had been his director father's.

Spunky, Melanie's black cat, was curled up in a tight ball on a chenille-covered sofa, acknowledging us with a languid blink as we entered.

"And how did the wedding-crasher cat enjoy the honeymoon cruise?" I asked as I went over to stroke his head with my fingertip. Spunky had followed us down the aisle at our wedding. He purred loudly at my touch. He is a cat I had rescued as a kitten a few years ago. But ungrateful beast, he had taken one long hard look into Melanie's eyes, which are so much like his own, recognized a kindred spirit and howled until I let her take him home. Where he has been treated like the prince of the feline world ever since.

"Spunky loves the yacht," Cam said, moving to the bar and selecting a decanter. "He sits up in the helm and watches the water, tail twitching. I can't imagine what he thinks he sees."

"But he did not like the plane trip back home," Melanie said. "I had to tranquilize him to get him to keep quiet, otherwise they would not have let me take him on board with me."

"Cam, what do you make of Brian's story about Citigroup and the Bellamy debt?" I asked as he passed out nightcaps.

"I've never heard anything about a purchasing agent working for Dr. Bellamy and the architects," Jon said. "This is a load of crap if you ask me."

"With purchases made so many years ago," Cam said reasonably, "anything is possible. Perhaps there was a purchasing agent. How complete are the records?"

"Not complete," I said. "Pieces missing. I do know that Dr. Bellamy paid the debt for the fourteen twenty-five foot columns to the Confederate Government, and then when the war ended, the Northern supplier sued for the cost of the columns. Dr. Bellamy paid that bill twice. I guess it is conceivable that some merchants, rather than carrying debts, sold their notes to a bank."

"That is not an uncommon business practice," Cam said.

Cam turned from the bar. He is tall and lanky, with unruly hair. He has a kind face. Everyone's favorite big brother.

"But who would ever imagine that Citigroup would somehow acquire the notes, or that they'd act to collect on them after a century and a half?" I said.

"Stranger things have happened," Cam said.

"Well, I know one thing," Melanie said. "If Brian tries to force the sale of the mansion with Candi and Han as the buyers, and me listed as the broker, people in this town will detest me so much I will never get another listing or make a sale. Folks here kind of believe that mansion belongs to the town, to the public. A place school children visit to learn about how life was lived a hundred and fifty years ago. It must remain a museum!"

"But what can you do?" Jon asked. "This is not your doing. You didn't know anything about the Bellamy Mansion's outstanding debts, did you?"

"No. Of course not," Melanie declared indignantly.

"Well, then, none of this was your doing," Jon said.

Melanie raged, "Do you think my enemies will believe that? No! I'll be screwed with every preservationist and community leader in this town. We're dependent on tourism, and if the Bellamy Mansion becomes a private residence and is no longer a tourist attraction, the tourist board will loathe me. My career will be over. Finished!"

"But like Jon said, Melanie, what can you do?" I asked. "You don't control Brian or the Chengs."

"There is no other house in the area that can compare with the Bellamy Mansion, so finding them a similar house is out of the question. No, somehow, I've got to find a way to stop them."

"Why don't they buy some land and build a replica of the Bellamy?" Jon asked.

"You know, I suggested just that to Candi. But no, she has to have an authentic antebellum mansion."

"Wait I minute," I said. "You didn't give Candi that beautiful blue jelly, did you?"

Melanie shook her head. "I wasn't about to present it to her at the party where it would get overlooked. I had planned to give it to her when we were alone."

"What's this about blue jelly?" Cam asked.

"It's a hand blown glass jelly fish," I said. "It's gorgeous, Cam. And called 'the Blue Moon.' I hope you are going to keep it," I told Melanie.

"I certainly do plan to keep it," she replied. "I'll find a bright sunny spot for it and feature it prominently. Maybe the garden room."

"Good. Because I think we are united in our repulsion for the Chengs. Not only are they trying to manipulate a local problem to their advantage to buy a landmark property that would not otherwise be available, but they are enemies of the environment." I told Jon and Cam about the contraband ivory and bigleaf mahogany.

"As incensed as we are, Jackie was even more livid. I doubt she will permit Brian to work with the Chengs."

"From the greedy look on Brian's face when he

described his fat fees, I doubt she'll be able to stop him," Cam said.

"Cam, we're delighted you're back, but you didn't explain how you…uhmmm, got away," I told my new brother-in-law.

"Yes, Cam. How is your mother?" Jon said.

What I really wanted to say was: How did you free yourself from the talons of the Dragon Lady? But I was raised well, so I kept my thoughts to myself.

Cam offered us another drink. "No thanks. I'm driving," Jon responded.

"I'm fine," I said.

Cam refilled his glass and returned to the sofa beside Melanie. After all, he was at home. And the subject of Nelda Cameron required fortification.

"Her cardiologist pronounced her fit as a fiddle," Cam said. "She argued, naturally, and feigned chest pains. But all of the tests showed her heart was healthy. They discharged her.

"And I got on the horn and hired her a nurse. He's about thirty-five and what you girls call a hottie!"

Cam's head fell back and he roared with laughter. "Thank god there's no sexism in the nursing profession. This man was very qualified and highly recommended. Mother forgot all about me." He snickered. "At least for the time being."

"I'm just glad you're home," Melanie said, leaning her head on his shoulder. "You were missed, darling."

"If you recall, I'm filming at the Bellamy Mansion in two weeks," Cam reminded us.

"How could I forget?" I said. "I'll be making my television debut on the special feature you're producing for 'Exploring North Carolina.'" "Exploring North Carolina" is a television show that runs on our PBS station, WUNJ-TV.

"I'm thinking about covering the belvedere restoration project, as well," Cam said. "I think our viewers would find it very interesting to see just how historic properties are restored."

"Sure," Jon said. "Let me know what you decide. We can work something out. How about playing golf in the morning? You up for that?"

"If it's all right with Melanie," Cam replied.

Melanie nodded. "You boys play golf. Ashley and I will go to church. We need to check on Aunt Ruby and Binkie."

"How did you like the courses in Pinehurst?" Cam asked Jon.

"Never got near them," Jon laughed. "My insatiable bride kept me locked in our suite. Only let me out long enough to eat. And that was to keep up my strength."

I swatted him on the arm. "Ouch," he cried, and pulled me into his arms for a hug.

EIGHT

On Sunday morning, Melanie and I attended church services at St. James Episcopal Church. St. James has been our family's church for generations. This was the first time we'd been back since our double wedding here on December twenty-second.

"We'll have a party soon to watch the video of the ceremony," Melanie said. "Out at the lodge. Maybe even have some of the wedding party join us. How's Saturday after next for you?"

"That's a great idea, Mel. I think we're free. I know we are. Want me to bring a casserole?"

Melanie snorted. "I remember your casseroles. Maybe we'd just better pick up some take out. Oh, look, here's Aunt Ruby and Binkie."

And I turned to see our Aunt Ruby and her husband Professor Benjamin Higgins approach our pew and then slide in with murmurs of greeting. Binkie had been my friend long before he and Aunt Ruby had rediscovered each other and began their long-distance courtship. In fact, Binkie had been like a father to both Melanie and me after our own father had died. Binkie was a history professor emeritus at UNCW. I realized that if anyone could fill in the voids on the monetary transactions that had occurred during the Civil War, Binkie would be the one. He is an expert on Lower Cape Fear history.

Binkie and Aunt Ruby are in their seventies. Aunt

Ruby will not permit a strand of gray hair on her head. And she wears makeup and stylish clothes. She says she owes her youthful figure to a daily two mile walk, despite rain or shine.

Binkie is more sedentary, very comfortable looking, with his tweedy jackets and soft corduroy slacks. He has silvery hair and crisp, intelligent blue eyes.

After services, we followed Aunt Ruby and Binkie out of the church. On the sidewalk out front, Aunt Ruby invited us to lunch. "I have the most wonderful news, girls," she said.

"We're due some good news," I said. "I'd love to come for lunch, Aunt Ruby. And I have some questions for you, Binkie."

He gave me a quick hug. "Always at your service, Ashley dear. My bride spent yesterday baking bread so we shall have the best sandwiches you girls have ever tasted."

"What about you, Melanie? Can you come?" Aunt Ruby asked.

"I can, Aunt Ruby. The boys are playing golf. I don't expect Cam home until mid-afternoon. We'll meet you at your house. I'll drive Ashley."

Since I live only several blocks from St. James, I always walk to church services.

"OK, meet you there," Aunt Ruby called.

"Come on, Ashley, this way," Melanie said, leading the way to her car. And I trailed along. Don't I always follow Melanie? She sees her role as the leader, and mine as the follower, and I am so pitiful, most times I fall lockstep right into my role. She drove south on Third, made a right turn and went over to Front Street to our Uncle Binkie's charming little bungalow that he had inherited from his mother.

Aunt Ruby was our departed mother's older sister, Ruby Chastain. As children, she and Binkie had been dance partners at the children's dances held at the spectacular, big band Lumina Pavilion on Wrightsville Beach prior to World War II. The beautiful old Pavilion is gone now, destroyed by hurricanes and forces of nature, and the community's failure to value their historic structures. Thankfully all that changed in the Seventies when preserving one's heritage was recognized as the right thing to do.

Ruby and Binkie had lived unmarried, solitary lives—he in Wilmington, she in Savannah—until they had met each other again last summer. Now they were grateful to be sharing their golden years as husband and wife.

We found parking spaces further down Front Street in front of the Governor Dudley mansion, and walked the block and a half back to Binkie's bungalow.

Aunt Ruby was waiting for us at the front door. "Come in, come in, my beautiful girls. Not that I would deny you your honeymoons but I am so happy that you are home again."

We hugged our aunt and she squeezed us, then we allowed ourselves to be steered down the narrow hallway into the parlor at the rear of the house. "You make yourselves comfy while I fix the sandwiches. Benjamin, would you pour tea for the girls.

"And now, bless my soul, we have another wedding to plan," she told us merrily as she disappeared into their small kitchen.

Melanie and I settled into Binkie's mother's antique

sofa and arm chair. We arched our eyebrows at each other as Binkie fussed over us and made small talk. "She has sworn me to secrecy," he said, beaming. "She wants the words to come only from her lips."

Wedding? Who did we know who was getting married?

"Now what did you want to discuss with me, Ashley dear?" Binkie asked.

Melanie got up. "I think I'll just go wash my hands." And she left us.

"Well, you know everything about our town's history," I began. "And Esther Hudson was telling Jon and me that during the antebellum period there was some conflict between the white carpenters and craftsmen and the African American carpenters. Can you shed some light on that?"

Binkie topped off my iced tea glass. "Esther is correct, Ashley. The African-Americans, both free and enslaved, were quite skilled in the building trades. They were craftsmen and artisans. They could accomplish things others could not. And they were free to bid their own contracts, as long as they gave a percentage to their owners. So they were able to underbid the whites. And they did.

"This often meant the white carpenters lost work. And they were outraged. Things got out of hand. One of the town leaders suggested that if they were unhappy with the system, they should leave town."

"And did they?"

Melanie returned.

Aunt Ruby called from the dining room, "Lunch is ready. Now y'all gather round the table and I'll tell you all about the wedding."

And we joined our aunt in their old-fashioned dining room with its heavy dark furniture and lace tablecloth. Most of the Chastain family furniture that had been in Aunt Ruby's house was now used in Melanie's house, with a few pieces in storage for me, waiting until when I could decide where I wanted to place them.

"Oh my, this looks scrumptious," I said as I eyed a sandwich of chicken salad, lettuce, and tomato on home baked thick, crusty whole wheat bread. On the side, there was fruit: sliced pears and red grapes.

"Grace first," Aunt Ruby directed. "Benjamin will you do the honors." And we joined hands as Binkie asked the blessing.

How his life has changed, I reflected. And how happy he looks. He loved being married to our aunt after a lifetime of bachelorhood spent in scholarly research, writing, and teaching. He once confided to me the sweetest thing, saying that he felt like he had been standing in the shade all of his life, until Aunt Ruby moved in and brought the sunshine with her. I was happy for both of them. Always happy when life turned out for the better, as mine had with Jon. Just the thought of him quickened my pulse.

"Enough of this mystery, Aunt Ruby," Melanie said. "What wedding? Whose wedding are we planning?"

"And why are *we* planning the wedding?" I asked. "We don't know anyone who is getting married."

"Well, land's sake, you just won't believe this. You could have knocked me over with a feather when I got the call. Now, just you settle yourselves while I fetch more tea, and then I'll tell you all the exciting news."

Aunt Ruby fluttered about, straightening napkins and the tablecloth, then flitted toward the kitchen.

Aunt Ruby does not flutter, nor does she flit, so this big mysterious wedding announcement had thrown her off kilter. Still, she seemed pleased by the news that someone was about to get married.

Aunt Ruby returned to the table with a fresh pitcher of raspberry tea.

"OK, Aunt Ruby, stop stalling. Who is getting married?" Melanie asked.

"Well, you will never believe this. But it is Scarlett and Ray. Isn't that grand? We were with them when they met. In fact, I was the one to introduce them. And we watched them fall in love."

"But Aunt Ruby," I said, astounded, setting my sandwich back on my plate, "that was just two weeks ago. How can they be getting married so soon? They barely know each other."

"I wonder, too," Melanie said. "What's the rush?"

Aunt Ruby sat up straighter in her chair and said in a serious tone, "Scarlett feels that she has wasted so much of her life while the FBI had her in the Witness Protection program. Now she's got her own life back again, and she and Ray are sure of their feelings for each other. She is forty, you know, not a child."

Scarlett Barrett was our older half-sister whom we had only met for the first time a little over two weeks ago when she appeared for our wedding. We would have met sooner but, as Aunt Ruby had just said, Scarlett had witnessed a murder important to a case the FBI was building, and they'd kept her in the Witness Protection program for six years—to ensure their case, and to ensure her safety.

"She's eager to get on with her life and to make up for those lost years," Aunt Ruby explained.

Melanie and I looked at each other. "I'm all for people claiming their happiness," Melanie said.

"Me too, Aunt Ruby. Count me in. Have they set a date? Will we all be going to New York?"

"They are insistent that the wedding be held here in Wilmington, girls. After all, we are Scarlett's only family now that the Barretts have passed. And they have set the date: Valentine's Day. Scarlett wants someplace very special."

"Oh, Valentine's Day will be so romantic," Melanie gushed. "I know, we can have a heart theme."

"I don't understand why they are not planning their own wedding," I said.

"Because, Ashley, we are here and they are not. Ray has got his hands full with the declining stock market. And Scarlett is busy going to auditions. True to her word, your mother-in-law, Melanie, Nelda Cameron called around and got Scarlett interviews with the most important producers."

So Nelda had made good on her promise to Scarlett. That's one brownie point for Nelda, I thought.

Our older half-sister Scarlett had been a Rockette before witnessing the murder which stole a huge chunk of years out of her life. She is a singer, a dancer, and an actress.

Ray is a future's trader, whatever that is, and the youngest member of the New York Stock Exchange. Ray's only living relative is his sister Kiki.

"Kiki will come, won't she?" I asked.

"Yes, Scarlett says she'll be here with bells on."

"Bells, indeed. That peculiar woman," Melanie huffed.

Kiki and I had shared an apartment with two other girls when we were students at Parsons School of Design in New York. Melanie had never been able to "get" Kiki although Kiki had gone on to become an internationally famous interior designer, the kind of woman Melanie ordinarily admired.

"With the economy the way it is right now," Melanie said, "the demand for lavish weddings isn't so great anymore. There will be cancellations. We should be able to find them a nice place."

"I know," I exclaimed. "The Bellamy Mansion. We'll hold it at the Bellamy Mansion."

"But darling girl," Aunt Ruby protested, "with that awful shooting of poor Willie, do we want to hold a wedding there? Our guests might be too frightened to attend."

"Nick assures me the PD is providing a strong uniformed police presence in the area," I said.

"Nick? Have you seen him?" Melanie wanted to know.

"Yes. He and that viperous Diane Sherwood came to our house on Friday to question us. As if we would know something about the shooting while we were miles away."

"The Bellamy Mansion *is* the perfect place to host a romantic wedding," Aunt Ruby said.

"Anyway," I said, "Willie doesn't have an enemy in the world. I think this shooting was just some psycho gun-nut who would have aimed for anyone who was up in the observatory. Or even on the ground. And surely by Valentine's Day they will have caught the shooter and life here will go back to normal."

"I wouldn't count on that happening," Melanie said.

NINE

LATER THAT SUNDAY AFTERNOON, Jon returned from his game, jubilant about his golfing prowess. He looked so cute in his golf shirt, and even cuter when he stripped to shower, that as soon as he was squeaky clean, I just had to cuddle with him. The cuddling escalated into the best kind of making out.

At four-thirty we headed out to the medical center to visit with Willie. On the drive, I told Jon about Scarlett and Ray's upcoming nuptials.

"Way to go, Ray!" he cried, punching the air. He turned to me and smiled, "We guys have to move fast if you want to tie the knot with one of you Wilkes girls. And don't I know that from experience. I delayed one second and you were snapped up."

AT THE MEDICAL CENTER we found Willie in a good mood, no longer fussy, memory recovered, and eager to tell all.

"The detectives have not been here yet today," Esther told us, "so you are the first outside of the family to hear all this."

Jon and I got settled in vinyl chairs and gave Willie our full attention.

"You sure are looking good for someone who was shot just four days ago," I said.

"The Hudson males always were handsome boys," he quipped. "Never had any trouble getting the girls."

Esther pretended to swat at him. "And praise the Lord, they've got hard heads."

"So tell us what you remember about that morning," Jon said.

"Well, I got to the mansion early, long before Lonnie and Dwayne put in an appearance. The caretaker was there, working over the holiday and he let me in. Said he was catching up and that anyway he had to open up for the party rental folks.

"See, there had been a New Year's Eve party at the Bellamy the night before. So the rental folks came early on New Year's Day to collect their tents, chairs and tables, and such. They were all out in the parking lot, loading the vans. But as I climbed those long stairs up to the roof, I came upon one of them. He seemed embarrassed to be caught wandering around the mansion on his own. He was coming down the stairs from the belvedere."

I was all ears. Who was this person? Were his motives as innocent as wanting to get a panoramic view from the top of the mansion? "Did you speak to him?" I asked.

"Yes. Asked him could I help him. He said, 'no,' he was just leaving. I asked him what he was looking for. He went on with some long song and dance 'bout how he was a history major at the university, and how he was just poking around hoping to see something of interest. Looked too old to be a college student to me. So, all the while he's backing away, and then he turned and ran back down the stairs.

"But when I got up into the belvedere and looked

down, I did not see him around the rental company vans. Still, he could have been inside, folding up the chairs, or whatever."

Esther handed him a large plastic cup and held it for him while he sipped water through a straw.

"What happened then?" Jon asked. I knew he wanted to know if Willie had seen the shooter.

"Well, up in the belvedere, I was paying no mind to the folks on the ground. I started prodding for dry rot, and believe you me I found aplenty. We have really got our work cut out for us, Jon, restoring those window frames."

"Yeah, it looked that way to Ashley and me when we gave the belvedere a cursory inspection right before the wedding," Jon replied.

"Anyway, I kinda lost track of time. Maybe about twenty minutes went by. I was making notes, and taking pictures. Drawing big Xs with white chalk on those windows that we definitely have to remove and take to the shop to rehab. Next thing I know, something kinda caught my peripheral vision. A flash. Motion."

He gave us a level look. "You know I wasn't facing that way. The next thing there was an explosion and it felt like something slammed me out of this world. Then nothing. Nothing till I woke up in this bed on Friday morning."

I reached over and squeezed his hand. "And we are so thankful you did wake up, Willie," I said. "It's a miracle that you made it."

"It sure is," Jon agreed.

"Praise the Lord," Esther said.

TEN

WE MET LONNIE HUDSON at the Bellamy Mansion early on Monday morning. The sun was up and shining brightly. The day would be sunny and dry, pleasant, a perfect day for working in the belvedere to resume the assessment that Willie had begun the day that he was shot.

"For eighteen-sixty, the plumbing system at the Bellamy was far ahead of its time," Lonnie told Jon and me as we ascended the stairs to the attic. He led us to the tank room on the third, or attic, floor. Lonnie was explaining how the system had functioned when the Bellamy family had moved into the house in February of eighteen-sixty-one, on the eve of the Civil War.

The tank room was a corner room on the attic level, tucked under the eaves at the rear of the house. With a low pitched roof and windows that were set about knee high, the room was cramped and gloomy. The tank itself was a large lead-lined reservoir, clad with oak planks. On display in the room was an old-fashioned sitz tub, but that would not have been where the Bellamys had bathed. In their day, the house had been equipped with a warm water shower in the bathroom directly below the tank room.

Lonnie explained, "Today this tank is as dry as dust because at some point the original plumbing system was replaced with city water. But way back when, the family got their drinking water from a well and their washing water from a cistern."

The well and cistern were unused now. The openings were sealed with heavy covers. And they were clearly visible in the rear yard.

"Warm water showers were unusual for that era," Jon said, "and as you say, well ahead of their time."

"Where did your great-great-grandfather learn how to construct such a sophisticated plumbing system since they were so uncommon?" I asked.

"Wilfred was a literate man," Lonnie boasted. "He learned to read as an adult. Then as a father, he taught his children to read. So all the Hudsons have been a literate family going back to the antebellum period.

"Wilfred found the plumbing design in a book written by a famous architect of the day. That's the way the story's been told in the family. And he was clever enough to know how to take that design and turn it into reality. And just like my pa, Wilfred relied on his sons and grandsons to assist him in his plumbing business."

I did not tell Lonnie that Willie had confided he was considering giving his son a greater role in running their general contractor's business. I'd let Willie do that. And Willie was right: Lonnie deserved a greater participation in running the operation.

"This is how the plumbing system worked back then," Lonnie told us. "The Bellamy butler, a young man named Guy who was a slave and also drove the carriage, would hand pump water from the cistern and force it up here to fill this tank." He indicated the boxy tank. "Down in the kitchen there was a large copper boiler. As needed, the water would flow down through pipes to the boiler where it was heated. Through a system of draw and stop cocks, the warm water flowed to wherever needed in the house. The bathroom was located under this tank room, so cold water could flow down there directly through a cold water pipe."

"You must be proud of your ancestors," I said.

Lonnie gave us an ah shucks grin. "I'm very proud of my family. The Hudsons have always been first rate citizens. We sent soldiers into every war, starting with the War for Independence."

"You have every reason to be proud," Jon said. "But we can't avoid the belvedere any longer. We need to go up there and view the damage from the shooting."

"I'll never forget finding my pa up there," Lonnie said with a shudder. "I dread going back up."

"Lonnie, I'll understand if you want to appoint someone else to handle this," Jon said kindly.

"No, no." Lonnie shook his head. "It's like getting back on a horse after you've been thrown. Or getting back on a plane after there's been a crash. It's something I've got to do. I'll be all right."

Jon clasped him on the shoulder. "I'm sure you will. OK, let's get this over with."

We were standing at the bottom of the stairwell to the observatory. The attic hallway was broad and had served as a play area for the Bellamy children. The children's bedrooms flanked either side of this floor as well, small rooms, one right after another. Dr. and Mrs. Bellamy had been blessed with ten children, nine of whom survived childhood and lived into adulthood.

There were windows in the hallway that admitted a paucity of light into the bedrooms. Then inside the bedrooms, there were floor-level windows that opened out under the eaves. Had the children found their rooms spooky, I wondered. They were spooky now. The rooms were now securely locked. Through the hallway windows one could see into the small rooms that were being used for storage.

In one room, lath was exposed. A project for a future day, I wondered. How could the museum ever raise seventy-five thousand dollars to pay off an old debt when it was hard pressed to raise funds for restoration?

At the far, south end of the attic floor, a loft area overlooked the Market Street side of the portico. Originally conceived to be used as a trunk room, the Bellamy children had appropriated the area for a doll house and a stage for plays. Now, as part of a museum, the platform held old-fashioned leather-bound trunks that would have been common to the Civil War period.

Jon led the way up the stairs to the belvedere. The staircase was very steep and narrow, the treads shallow. He stepped out onto the landing while Lonnie and I mounted the steps. There was a railing at the edge of the landing that separated the rooftop chamber from the stairwell. A second, security railing had been erected to bolster the original railing which had come lose with age and the many hands that had grasped it for support.

Instantly I saw the damage that the shooter had caused. The floor of the belvedere was littered with glass where the bullet had shattered one pane on the south side. The bullet had then passed through the belvedere, wounding Willie's skull before exiting through another glass pane on the north side.

And darkening the litter of glass shards was the rusty brown stain of Willie's dried blood.

Lonnie followed Jon into the belvedere, and seemed subdued. "Head wounds bleed profusely, one of the nurses told us," he said sadly.

"The caretaker who let me in told me the cops found the bullet. They followed its trajectory and found it lodged high in a tree trunk over near the slave quarters. Only one bullet. People in the neighborhood said they heard only one shot fired. The forensics guys theorized that the shooter must have feared that firing a second bullet would attract attention and he had to make a quick getaway."

Lonnie turned to me with sorrowful eyes as he politely gave me a hand while I stepped up onto the landing. "One shot and he almost killed my pa."

I reached out and rubbed his arm.

"This is worse than I imagined," I said. "What do you think, Jon?"

Jon was trying not to look at the blood, as was I. "We've got two window panes to replace," he said. "I think if we search the salvage yards we might get lucky and find a sash with glass panes from the same period. Then we can get a glass cutter to cut the panes to size to fit into our muntins."

"Mason has trained as a glazier," Lonnie offered.

"That's great, Lonnie. We can use his help," Jon said.

"We've got sills, stiles, and rails to repair," I said, eyeing the wood rot. "The exterior frames are in good shape because they were painted periodically." The entire house had been painted its original pristine white fairly recently.

"Probably these louvers will have to be replaced, as well," Jon said, indicating moveable louvers that were set low in the wall which adjusted automatically to let cool air into the attic.

For all its beauty, the belvedere served a most important practical function. On hot days, the lower sashes in the windows in the main rooms of the house would be raised. The open sashes in the belvedere would draw breezes from the lower floors through the rooms, up the stairways, and out through the belvedere, creating circulating, cooler air. Then, in the Nineties, central air conditioning had been installed.

The light was brilliant up here as the sun shone through the twelve arched windows. I could see far into the distance. The historic district was spread out below us, and to the west the Cape Fear River rippled and sparkled as it flowed south. The belvedere lived up to its name: beautiful view. Now this fair lookout had been sullied by the attempted murder and near death of our good friend. I clenched my fists. I was deeply angry. What a senseless deed, I kept thinking to myself.

As we moved about the belvedere, every step we took resulted in the crushing and grinding of glass beneath our boots.

"I've got a broom and dust pan, and a big plastic garbage can out in my truck," Lonnie said. "I'll go fetch them and we'll get to work cleaning up this glass. We don't want to be tracking glass shards through the house with our boots, and nothing can be done up here until we clean up my poor pa's blood."

"Good idea," Jon said. "Ashley and I will help. Then we'll try to look on the positive side: Willie is going to be fine, and we've got a satisfying task begging for our attention."

Lonnie moved toward the stairs. I turned to stare

out of the shattered window across the intersection of
Market and Fifth to the Carolina Apartments. Far below,
in the middle of the intersection, the Kenan Fountain
plashed water merrily. The apartment building was one
of the few structures as tall as the Bellamy Mansion.
With a scope on a rifle, the shooter would have had an
unobstructed view of the belvedere. Anyone up here
would have been a sitting duck for an ace shooter who
had his heart set on murder.

As Nick had said, the area had been saturated with
uniformed police officer presence. I'd seen them as
we'd driven to the Bellamy.

I was deep in thought, trying to make sense of a
tragedy that made no sense. No one hated Willie. He
was respected and admired. And loved by many.

The next thing I knew I heard a crash. I wheeled
around to see the railing crashing down the stairwell.
And Lonnie sliding down the stairs under the fallen
stair rail.

ELEVEN

"THAT RAILING WAS tampered with!" Jon exclaimed. He and I were trapped in the belvedere while Lonnie lay moaning on the stairs. He too was trapped by the sections of railing that had fallen on him.

We had called 911 and already could hear sirens approaching from a distance.

"I can see that the railing has been tampered with," I said, as I crunched over shattered glass to hunker down next to the broken railing.

I looked down at Lonnie. He was conscious, eyes darting. "The ambulance is on its way," I said.

"Don't move, Lonnie," Jon called down. "You could have a fracture."

"I don't think I broke a bone," Lonnie called. "I'm just afraid to move because I've got these broken pickets poking at me every which way."

"OK, don't move. The paramedics will get you out. Someone did this on purpose," Jon said.

I peered closely at the stubs of the old pickets "You can see where they unscrewed the bolts that held the reinforcement railing in place. And they sawed through the old pickets. We would have seen this if we had been looking. But we were too focused on the blood and broken glass to notice." Then I said to Lonnie, "You must have grabbed the railing when you started down the stairs."

"Yeah, I did that automatically," Lonnie replied. "Like I always do. Force of habit. Grabbed onto the railing and started down. Next thing I knew, the whole blame thing came apart and was hitting my head and shoulders. Then the big rail came down and trapped me under it. Now I've got these sawed off pickets poking at me and I'm afraid to move."

From our vantage point in the belvedere, I saw the ambulance pull into the parking lot. The siren stopped its yelping and there was blessed silence. Two volunteers come out of the gift shop, staring at the ambulance in awe and puzzlement. In seconds, racing footsteps and loud voices on the lower staircase announced the arrival of the paramedics.

"Up here," I called. "We're up here."

In seconds the paramedics pulled the demolished railing pieces from off Lonnie and threw them into a pile in the hallway. While one EMT took Lonnie's blood pressure, shone a light in his eyes, and asked him questions, the other felt his limbs for breaks. In another minute, they had a cuff around Lonnie's neck, somehow maneuvered him onto a stretcher, and were carrying him down the stairs.

"We'll follow you to the medical center, Lonnie," I called.

"No, you won't. You've got some questions to answer," a familiar voice called from below.

Jon and I looked at each other. "Oh, no," I groaned. And we went down the stairs to find Nick waiting for us.

"Have you become an ambulance chaser?" I asked, as I thought how grateful I was that Nick was alone and

Diane Sherwood did not seem to be here to fawn over him on this occasion.

He ignored my sarcasm. Without his habitual sunglasses I could at least see his eyes. He looked very worried, and that gave me a shock.

"Are you all right?" Nick asked and grasped me by the shoulders.

I shook off his hands. "I'm fine. It's Lonnie who fell. Jon and I," and I stressed the name Jon, "are fine."

"What were you doing up there?" Nick growled.

"We work here. Remember?" Jon responded.

Nick paused for a second and stared at us. "Yeah, right."

Then he turned his back on us and paced down the hallway to a midpoint where he stopped. He seemed to straighten up a little taller, and braced his shoulders. Then he turned and retraced his steps back toward us. What in the world was going on with him?

"OK. When I heard the call on the scanner for an ambulance here at the mansion, I decided to check it out."

Now he was back in his cop's mode.

He continued, "I didn't know what I was going to find here but since you and Jon are involved with this project, I wanted to see for myself what was going on. I didn't expect to…well, I'm glad you and Jon are not injured. Now, tell me exactly what happened here?"

Jon reminded Nick that we were going to restore the belvedere, and that to do so we had to assess the damage from the shooting. Then he told Nick that Lonnie grabbed the handrail and started down the steps only to have the entire rail fall apart and crash into the stairwell, throwing Lonnie off balance and causing him to fall.

"This was no accident," Jon stated. "Someone sabotaged the reinforcement railing and sawed through the pickets. This was deliberate."

Nick circled the stack of broken railing, then kicked at it. "I can see that. I doubt there will be any useful fingerprints with so many hands touching this thing, but I'll have the CSU guys take a look anyway."

I remembered something. "Nick, Willie told us he caught one of the rental equipment guys roaming around up here the morning he was shot."

"Yeah, Hudson told me the same thing. We're looking into that," Nick responded with disinterest.

Then he gave us a thoughtful look. "You know, when Hudson was shot, I thought this was all about him. Someone with a grudge against Hudson. But now? Well, I am reassessing our perp's motives. Looks to me like he's trying to shut down this project. Someone does not want you restoring that observatory. Why would anyone want to do that?" He looked from Jon to me.

I replied, "Nick, that doesn't make sense. Why would anyone care enough to prevent us from restoring the belvedere?"

"That is what I'm asking you, Ashley."

"Well, I don't know."

"What other explanation is there?" Nick asked.

"You're the detective, Nick," I said.

"And you're always the victim!" he retorted savagely.

Jon had said nothing during this exchange. Now he said, "Nick, we used to be friends. Now all we get from you is hostility."

"That's true, Nick," I said. "Why are you so hostile?"

Nick's jaw tightened with suppressed rage. "Because, dammit, that could have been you up there, grabbing the broken hand rail and falling down those stairs! And that could have been you in the belvedere when a sharpshooter went on a shooting rampage! You little fool, you're always so careless. And then you find yourself in danger. And you expect me to come rescue you!"

His intensity alarmed me.

"Now," he threatened, "I've got a good mind to shut down this project until we catch this guy."

"You can't do that," I yelled at him.

"Oh yes, I can, baby. In the interest of public safety I can declare this mansion off limits until we've got our perp locked up securely behind bars!"

TWELVE

"NICK IS STILL in love with you, Ashley," Jon told me over dinner. I did not detect resentment in his statement. Nor jealousy. Jon is much too confident about what he has to offer to be jealous of another man.

He gave me one of his special looks. It's the one where his face lights up and his eyes look deeply into mine, so that I experience again our connection and the joy that passes between us. Plus the raw animal magnetism. "Not that I blame him. Only an idiot would let you go."

"Oh, Jon, I don't think so. Nick just lets himself get so wrapped up in a case that he can't think straight. I lived with him, remember? I know how he can be."

But secretly I agreed with Jon. Nick was still in love with me. I had seen it in his eyes. But I would never, ever admit that to Jon.

"Ashley, I'm glad Nick didn't have the good sense to appreciate what he had until it was too late. For two years I played the role of your best bud. Waiting for you to open your eyes and see me. Waiting for you to grow up, I suppose.

"I was grateful to Nick when he went off the deep end and got caught up in that Blackwater Security misadventure. Thought he was some sort of super-hero but all he ever was was just another hired gun. Went to Iraq with those outlaws and didn't even tell you where he was going. Nick's a dope."

He gave me one of his heart melting smiles. "But I'm glad he's a dope. Because of his idiocy I got the chance to show you how good we could be together. We want the same things out of life. The universe is a better place because we are together. This is just so right."

I reached across the table and stroked his hand. "I couldn't agree more. So let's forget about Nick and not spoil this wonderful dinner with talk of him. It's bad enough he keeps turning up with his investigation. Now, how about refilling my wine glass."

WE HAD SPENT HOURS at the medical center emergency room while Lonnie was checked over and X-rayed. Even though his parents were right there in the same hospital, Lonnie would not permit anyone to phone them, or any members of his family.

"My folks have been through enough," he said. "I'll be just fine and I don't want to cause any more worries for my family. No more bad news, and scaring my poor mother half to death."

And the doctors agreed that he was uninjured. Just some bumps and bruises. Jon and I drove him home where he promised to stay put with his feet up for a day or two.

IN THE EVENING Jon and I walked down Nun Street to the riverfront for a casual dinner at Le Catalan, a really neat wine bar. The breeze off the river was nippy, and daylight had faded an hour earlier. But we strolled hand-in-hand and when we reached the riverfront, we both felt invigorated from the exercise. And hungry.

The café's décor had a theme: wine bottle corks.

Wine bottle corks served as the crown molding, chair rail, and delineated architectural features. Just inside the front door, a darling little man made of wine corks sat in a chair, greeting guests with his adorable painted smile, and proudly sporting a white chef's hat.

For dinner, we ordered my favorite, Le Catalan's specialty for a wintry evening, Beef Bourgignon with a bottle of good French red wine. The service here was always excellent, plus warm and friendly. In the spring we would sit outside on the boardwalk, and I longed for warm weather.

At first we had talked about the changes we were going to make to my house—now our in-town house—to accommodate us as a couple. We were avoiding the topic of Lonnie's fall down the stairs and the booby trap that had been set for him. Or for one of us. Then Jon sprang his declaration that Nick was still in love with me.

Jon topped off my wine glass and I took a sip. "My love for Nick was a shallow thing compared to my love for you," I said softly. "He gave me a quarter of himself. You give me all of yourself. You put our life together first. Before work, friends, everything. And that is what I need and what I want to give in return. So let's just forget about Nick, except to pity him."

"I do pity him," Jon said. "But I'm afraid that we're going to be involved with him for as long as this investigation goes on."

"Do you really think that he has the power to shut down the museum and our restoration project?" I asked.

"I seriously doubt the mayor would let him. Everyone knows how important the Bellamy Mansion Museum is to the tourist economy. About all they can do is beef up security," Jon responded.

"I think you're right. You know the saying 'No good deed goes unpunished.' That is about how I feel right now. We try to do the right thing and volunteer our expertise and services to restore the belvedere, and what happens? A good friend gets shot, and the railing is jimmied so someone will fall. What else is going to happen? And why?"

I pushed my plate away, no longer hungry. Nick was right about one thing. That could have been me who fell down those stairs. Or Jon. Or the caretaker. Or one of the staff. Or a volunteer. And they could have been seriously injured.

"Could any of this have to do with the Chengs?" I asked. "They are dead set on buying the mansion. Could this be some ploy to scare everyone off? To create so much bad publicity for the Bellamy, causing it to be so unappealing as a museum, that Preservation NC would jump at the chance to sell it?"

"That thought occurred to me, too," Jon said. "But I just can't imagine anyone being so desperate to buy a house, they'd be willing to kill for it."

I leaned forward and lowered my voice. A couple was seated just two tables away. We four were the only patrons in the restaurant on a slow Monday evening. And in the quiet, conversations carried. "But what do we know about them? Nothing. They're filthy rich. We know they don't give a darn about the environment or about God's creatures. In my experience, people that rich have rarely acquired their wealth through ethical means. Oh, of course, there are exceptions. Bill Gates for instance. But that Candi is a piece of work.

Self-centered and arrogant. She can't see any further than her own nose and her own wants and wishes. And Han acts like winning is the only thing that matters to him."

"Han is very caught up in success," Jon agreed. "I'm not sure what he's doing here or exactly how he is involved with the new port deal, but he is determined that the deal go through. He's got that fleet of container ships that require a deeper port."

"I'll bet he's here to do some arm twisting," I speculated. "And he's got plenty of money to grease the wheels of progress."

"Let's change the subject and talk about something sweet," Jon said with a smile, and signaled the waitress that he was ready for the dessert menu.

"Don't tempt me," I said, and meant it.

"OK, I'll skip dessert so you won't be tempted." And he set the dessert menu off to the side.

"I've gained another pound," I said. "And I feel like I'm starving myself. I'm as irritable as a bear."

Jon paid the check and stood up. The other couple were pulling on coats and leaving, as well. "OK, mama bear, how about a short walk on the boardwalk, then we'll head home. I have the perfect cure for your irritability." He helped me with my coat and said into my ear, "Guaranteed to make you purr."

I buttoned my winter coat and gave him a wink. "Come on, let's go look at the stars."

We left the wine bar by the river side exit. Outside the night was clear and crisp. We walked north on Riverwalk along the swiftly flowing Cape Fear River. The moon sparkled on the water. The stars were out and only a few people strolled the boardwalk.

"This is very romantic," I said as I reached inside his coat to wrap my arms around his waist and snuggle his warm body. He kissed me. Gently at first, then urgently until he took my breath away. I felt overwhelmed by my sudden need for him.

"I've never been happier, Jon. Even with the scary things happening at the mansion, I'm still happy."

"Me, too, Ashley. A short walk and then home to bed. The best part of the day is that when it ends, we go home together."

We walked as far as Riverfront Park, then turned around and retraced our steps. "I love our town when it is quiet like this. I know we need the tourists, but I'm selfish. I like having the river, this boardwalk, the entire downtown, all to ourselves."

He hugged me around the shoulders. "And I love having you all to myself."

Then he went on, seriously now. "You know, Ashley, I've been thinking about what you asked: could the Chengs be behind these attempted murders. And I have to say, I can't rule them out. I've never had any business dealings with Brian Hudson either. I only know him as a party animal. I wonder how ethical he is. Could all that falderal about foreclosure based on some ancient bank note be a scam to coerce Preservation NC into selling the Bellamy?"

"I've wondered that myself," I said. "Until I see those documents with my own eyes, I won't believe his story."

We exited Riverwalk and started up the hill at Nun Street. The enormous ballast wall rose to our right. "But if he takes a lien, wouldn't he have to produce the original bank notes?" I wondered out loud.

"Seems that way to me, too," Jon replied. "Who knows that they didn't cook up some forgeries?"

At the top of the hill stood the Governor Dudley house, facing Front Street. We paused at the corner, looked both ways beyond the parked cars and started across. From out of nowhere, car headlights caught us in their glare. The car bore down on us, swiftly, aiming straight for us with no attempt to stop.

The lights shone brightly on us in the middle of the street. The driver had to see us. But he sped onward toward us, accelerating and closing the distance. If anything, the car was moving faster.

Jon grabbed my arm and we sprinted to the far side of the street. He was shouting obscenities at a driver we could not see in the darkness, propelling me with one arm, shaking his fist at the driver with the other. I have never heard him swear like that or seen him so furious.

At the curb, I lost my footing and fell onto my knees. Jon lifted me to my feet. "Ashley, sweetheart, are you all right? That idiot! He could have hit us."

Then I saw Jon's face in the streetlight. And I saw how fear contorted his handsome features. "That was deliberate," he said.

THIRTEEN

"My slacks are heavy and protected my knees," I said. "Still they don't feel too steady."

"Aunt Ruby is only a block away. She's a nurse. We'll go there." And he swept me up into his arms and carried me like I was a baby.

Aunt Ruby took one look at us through the glass storm door and instantly let us in. "What happened?" she asked. "Bring her back to the parlor, Jon." She called out, "Benjamin, would you fetch my first aid kit, please, dear."

She led the way down the narrow hallway to the parlor at the rear of their cozy little bungalow. "Put her on the sofa, Jon. Ashley dear, can you get your coat off?"

"I fell on my knees, Aunt Ruby. My arms of fine." And I shrugged off my coat.

"Let's take a look," Aunt Ruby said, while turning on extra lamps. "Slide your slacks up, dear." And I did. A worried Binkie and Jon peered over her shoulder.

"Your knees are red. They will probably bruise. But I don't see any scrapes. I'm going to feel around a bit. Holler, if something hurts."

But nothing did hurt as she gently prodded my knees and shins. "Just tender," I said. "I'll be all right."

"Stay put for a while. I've got some cold packs in the freezer. We'll apply those to reduce any swelling."

Binkie brought the cold packs and Aunt Ruby had me stretch out my legs so that she would apply them to my knees.

"Feels good," I said.

"Benjamin, why don't you break out the sherry," Aunt Ruby asked. She is the only person who called Binkie by his given name. While he assembled sherry glasses on a tray, and removed the decanter stopper, Aunt Ruby urged, "Now tell us what happened. Surely you were not up in that belvedere at this hour."

"Oh no. I tripped on the curb, is all. I'm just a klutz," I said. "Tripped over my own big feet."

I gave Jon a warning look, but that was not necessary. He knew better than to tell them about two accidents in one day, or that Lonnie and I were both banged up.

As we sipped our sherry, Jon raised the subject of Brian Hudson's claim that there were outstanding debts owed by Preservation NC on behalf of the Bellamy Mansion. "Do you think this is true, Binkie? Could there have been debts that were never paid?"

Binkie settled gracefully into his favorite chair, a chintz-covered arm chair that had not changed since his mother had brought it into this room decades ago. "Anything is possible, Jon. Those were complex times. The Confederate government was collecting monies owed to Northern merchants, and then when the South lost the war, the merchants sued and debtors had to pay again. I presume you have heard that Dr. Bellamy was obligated to pay twice for those colossal Corinthian columns that surround three sides of the mansion. The sequestrian officer here in Wilmington, DuBrutz Cutlar, condemned that debt and Dr. Bellamy was forced to pay the outstanding sum to the Confederate government. Then after the war, the firm of Jenkins & Porter in New York sued Dr. Bellamy, and he was required to again pay the sum of about sixteen hundred dollars for the columns."

Jon said, "Ashley and I are watching Ken Burns' documentary on the Civil War. We're trying to refresh our memories about the details of that tragic war, when not only the nation, but even families were divided. Four million men fought in that war; six hundred thousand of them died. It was a calamity."

"Daddy used to always say that slavery was a great evil," I said.

"Wilmington got off easy compared to some towns," Binkie said. "And the gold that poured through this town! The war caused inflation, so goods and services were 'dear' as they used to say."

"How much did it cost Dr. Bellamy to build his mansion?" Jon asked.

Binkie got up to refill our small sherry glasses. When he had settled back in his chair, he responded, "We don't know for sure, Jon. Not all of the records are available. Some quote a figure of twenty-one thousand dollars. But Dr. Bellamy's son, John D. Bellamy, Jr., told the newspaper that the construction costs exceeded fifty thousand dollars. That would be based on the pre-war economy. Inflation ran rampant during the war years. Thus, the house would have been valued at considerably higher in only a few years. Consider this, Jon, the Confederacy levied a War Tax on the house that amounted to about twenty-two thousand dollars. So if the construction bill was a mere twenty-one thousand, he paid more in taxes than it cost to build the house."

"Brian Hudson told us that the unpaid banknote plus interest, penalties, and legal fees will amount to approximately seventy-five thousand dollars. Do you think that is possible?"

Binkie stroked his chin. "From what I've learned about this bank bailout—the TARP as they are calling it—what Brian says seems correct. Those banks that cannot collect on their bad debts may be impossible to save, thus permitted to fail. Those that can collect may be entitled to loans from the government to tide them over."

"We've both been trying to understand the economic straits the country finds itself in," Aunt Ruby said. "The banks are downsizing personnel in order to reduce overhead, so it may be true that they are outsourcing the collection process. That part of Brian's scenario seems plausible."

Binkie voiced what we were all thinking. "But whether a Northern bank bought up Dr. Bellamy's debts from New York merchants through a purchasing agent…well, that remains to be seen. It might not be too difficult to register a lien, but I expect it would not be easy to force the sale of the mansion."

Aunt Ruby said, "Ashley, Jon, we want you to take great care while you are working in that belvedere. Is there some way to ensure your safety? Benjamin and I are mighty worried about you two. We couldn't love you more if you were our own children."

Jon blinked back tears. He adored my aunt and her darling husband.

"Don't worry, Aunt Ruby," he said, leaning forward to touch her knee. "With about a day's work, we will remove the sashes and take them to the shop to be rehabbed. The empty window frames will then be filled in with plywood. I'll make sure that all of the windows facing the Carolina Apartments are covered with plywood first. Then if someone should attempt to fire at us from a high window, their bullets will hit only plywood. And the Carolina Apartments is the only tall building within shooting distance of the belvedere."

"That is a good solution, Jon," Binkie said. "But what about when you are working on the exterior? Won't you be especially vulnerable at that time?"

Jon hastened to reassure them. "The exterior is in good shape. We won't have to go out there."

"Thank heavens for that," Aunt Ruby said. "Now, you must be very, very careful on the day you are removing the sashes and installing the plywood."

"That should be done by the end of the week, weather permitting. And I will insist that the police search the empty apartments and post a uniformed officer in the lobby. After all, this is a matter of public safety."

Clever Jon. He was going to turn Nick's threat to our advantage.

"Thank you for reassuring us old folks, Jon," Aunt Ruby said with a smile.

THAT NIGHT, Jon made love to me with an intensity we had never experienced before. "You are my life, Ashley," he said softly. "If anything ever happened to you I wouldn't want to go on living. I fell in love with you almost the first time I saw you. I remember exactly when it happened. We were restoring Reggie Campbell's house. You came in dressed in khaki shorts and a white tee shirt. You had a yellow hard hat on your head with curls spilling out around it. And a bulky tool belt strapped around your waist. The tool belt was so big and you were so petite, I thought it would pull you down. God, you were cute. I took one long thirsty look into those huge lavender eyes of yours, and I was lost. I felt clumsy and tongue-tied, and totally turned on."

"Like you are now?" I asked, caressing him in the darkness.

"Just like I am now. I was so hungry for you I didn't know what to do with myself."

"I know what to do with you," I whispered.

And I did.

FOURTEEN

ON THURSDAY, Melanie met me at the Bellamy Mansion. As usual she was in a whirl, running between one house showing and the next. She was dressed to the nines in a fitted cream-colored wool suit with a short skirt, brown croc high heels, and the double strand of fine family pearls Mama had so lovingly given to her shortly before her hospitalization in a memory-care facility. On that autumn afternoon, which in some ways seems like a lifetime ago, and in other ways seems like only yesterday, Mama had briefly been restored to her old self. She had seized the opportunity for clear thinking to divide the family jewelry between Melanie and me and had presented me with Great-aunt Lillian's rubies.

Our mother had been diagnosed with Alzheimer's disease at an early age and lasted only a few years after that. Daddy was already gone. Melanie and I had only each other until Aunt Ruby married Binkie and moved to Wilmington. And now we had Scarlett for a sister, and would soon have Ray for a brother. And, of course, we now had our cherished husbands. The road to happiness sometimes takes a rocky detour, but what really mattered was that we had reached a perfect destination.

Melanie set her briefcase down on the dark pink floral carpeting in the mansion's front parlor and pulled out a notebook and a pen. "We've got five weeks to plan a wedding. I've started working on the guest list. Scarlett called and said I should plan that, too."

From high in the mansion the faint sound of hammering drifted down to the first floor.

"Honestly, Ashley, the nerve. Whose wedding is this anyway? Scarlett and Ray's? Or mine? You'd think it was mine. But hey! Been there, done that!"

"You planned mine too, remember, Mel? Our double wedding was fabulous. Without you, I would never have been able to pull off such a spectacular wedding. It was perfect. Scarlett knows how talented you are. And capable. That is why she is leaving all the details to you. Who else could do it better?"

I was intent on creating peace within our little family that had only recently grown to admit a step-sister we had never known existed.

Melanie preened and got a self-satisfied expression on her face. "It's true. I can pull this off better than anyone else. Now where's that wedding planner? I got her name from Candi. She planned the party on Candi's yacht. And with such short notice we are lucky to get her. She's supposed to be here now. And Elaine is on her way. At least Elaine is someone we can count on."

Elaine was a caterer who had been Melanie's friend since high school. She had catered our wedding reception. She was tops. No one could out cook Elaine.

I had not told Melanie about Jon's and my near miss out on Front Street from a potential hit-and-runner on Monday evening. Nor had we told anyone about Lonnie's rigged accident on the stairs. For one thing we were trying to protect the Bellamy's reputation. But the public, being composed of perverse individuals, had flocked to the Bellamy Museum in record numbers. The number of visitors touring the mansion had increased ever since the news got out that someone had shot into the belvedere. Bookings for parties and weddings had increased. The shooting and what you'd normally expect to be bad publicity only attracted people to the scene of the crime. Again I thought how difficult it was to get a handle on human nature.

But Melanie was off and running about her own problems. "When will this dreadful recession end?" she groaned. "Ahh, the sales I have lost. Still, were it not for the recession and that groom losing his job so that they had to scale down their wedding, we would not have been able to get the Bellamy Mansion on such short notice. And on Valentine's Day. The director said they are always rented out for Valentine's Day."

"I hate the economic downturn, too," I said. "It's just as well Jon and I are involved with this volunteer project. I don't know if we'd be able to pick up a big, paying restoration project just now. It's like someone pushed the 'pause' button. People are just holding their breaths. But we'll have a new president in a couple of weeks, and then I think things will start to improve."

"I think you are right. About the only real client I've got these days is Candi Cheng. The rest are just window shopping. Looking for a steal. And despite what I tell clients, that is rare. Unless the sellers are really desperate, or it's a foreclosure property, which in most cases is trashed property…well, the owners of good houses are just biding their time until the market upswings again."

"It'll pick up," I said. "After all, people have got to live somewhere."

"Ohmygosh! I almost forgot. Ray and Scarlett want me to find them a beach house. They'll continue to live in Ray's townhouse in New York, of course, but they'll fly down for long weekends and holidays. Won't that be great? Maybe Ray can give me some stock tips. There must be some stock worth buying these days."

Ray was a future's trader on Wall Street, the youngest member of the New York Stock Exchange. Very successful. Very rich. Very good looking. Very nice.

"That's great news, Mel. We'll get to see them often. We can all go out to their beach house in the summer and have parties. I can't wait to see them again.

"You know, Scarlett and Ray are lucky to have found each other," I continued, thinking about how my love for Jon was developing many facets: passion of course, but tenderness, and protectiveness. He was up in the belvedere right now, inserting plywood panels into the apertures.

I walked over to the parlor's southeast window and gazed out at the garden. The first floor windows rose to a little over nine feet tall. They were called "hollow-head" windows, constructed so that the bottom sash slid up into a pocket above the window head, thus creating a portal through which persons could step through to the piazza. Immense magnolia trees surrounded the house, shading and cooling it during our long, hot summers.

"There's Elaine," I called to Melanie as I watched Elaine's van pull into the parking lot. "She's brought her assistant."

"Oh, you mean Kimberly. Such a sweet girl. So eager to please."

Melanie came to stand behind me; together we watched Elaine and Kimberly climb down out of the cab of the catering van. After Elaine's husband Larry's death, she was forced to take on an assistant to fulfill many of the duties he had once performed.

Elaine and Kimberly came in through the back and immediately Elaine went to Melanie and gave her a big hug. Then one for me. Elaine is a plump, motherly sort of woman with wild curly hair. She has raised her capacity for nurturing to an art form through cooking and serving the most divine food. Kimberly hung back, but when we greeted her she joined our circle.

"I've hired Vanessa Holder to be the wedding planner. And where is she? I'll probably get stuck doing all the work," Melanie complained. "But at least she can coordinate the arrangements with the Bellamy staff, and relay my instructions to the vendors." She tapped a toe on the floral carpeting. "If she doesn't get here in five minutes, she's fired before she starts!"

"Vanessa Holder, the wedding planner?" Elaine said. "I've worked with her before. A bit overbearing for my tastes, but basically she's OK. She's rather pretentious."

"Well, she'd just better not be overbearing on my time," Melanie rejoined.

"Kimberly's got some suggestions for the menu. She was up half the night researching the Valentine's theme. Go ahead, Kimberly, tell her."

Kimberly stepped forward shyly. She was about four years younger than me, about twenty-two. With dark honey-colored flyaway hair and hazel eyes. Tawny complexion. Medium height and wiry. Elaine had told us she had graduated from UNCW in December with a degree in computer science. A very poor girl from West Virginia, Elaine had explained, who had paid her way through college with part-time jobs and student loans. She was now looking for a job in her field and supporting herself with the same part-time jobs.

Now Kimberly said, softly at first, but then warming to her subject, so that it became obvious she put her heart into her work. "We'll serve the food from a big tent. I thought we'd go with the love theme. If you approve we could start off with an oyster bar. We'll serve oysters on the half shell from a bed of chipped ice. We can get the oysters from Southport or Calabash. You know February has an 'r' in it and oysters are to be eaten in months with an 'r.'"

"Oysters! Oh, I love it. The men will all associate them with aphrodisiacs and just wolf them down," Melanie said. Then chuckled suggestively. "Especially my man." She got another one of her pleased with herself smiles and said, "Not that he needs any help."

I was so glad their marriage was working out and that Melanie was happy. Good for Melanie and Cam. They were making it, despite both having big-time careers and Cam's burdensome mother whom, happily, they had not heard from in a week.

Melanie regarded Kimberly with renewed respect. "Good idea, Kimberly. What else do you have in mind?"

"I've planned the entire menu around aphrodisiacs and ingredients related to love," Kimberly said, warming up and losing her shyness. "We'll have tomatoes with mozzarella and basil."

"Tomatoes are aphrodisiacs?" I said.

Kimberly ducked her head, then lifted defiant eyes to peer at me through long bangs. "Yes, ma'am. Those

French folks refer to tomatoes as love apples." Had she become a mite defensive?

Uh oh. A sensitive creature. I was going to have to be careful and not appear to be challenging her.

FIFTEEN

"STOP INTERRUPTING, ASHLEY," Melanie warned. "Kimberly knows what she's doing."

Kimberly beamed, her skin flushing red.

After that I kept my mouth shut. This was Melanie's show and if she was happy, I was happy. Besides I had other things on my mind. There had not been any homicidal attempts since Monday. Three days without an episode. I was keeping my fingers crossed. My bruised knees were healing up just fine.

"Then we'll have cucumber salad," Kimberly was saying. "The scent of cucumbers is supposed to be a turn on for women. Personally, I don't see it, but that's what the food experts say. And we'll serve asparagus with hollandaise sauce. Caviar topped roasted new potatoes. Eggs are an obvious fertility symbol."

I wondered to myself if Scarlett was interested in having children. I doubted that Melanie did. Spunky, the cat, was her baby.

"We'll have shrimp with garlic, both considered aphrodisiacs in many cultures. For dessert there will be chocolate covered strawberries. We'll have wine, of course, but we'll also serve ginseng tea, because the ginseng root looks like a…" At this point Kimberly covered her mouth and giggled. "A 'you know what'. They call it the 'man root'," she explained.

Melanie raised her eyebrows at Kimberly's naiveté. "Let's talk about the wedding cake," she said.

"If you want," Kimberly went on, "I could have menu cards printed up describing the aphrodisiacal properties in each of the ingredients we're serving."

"That's a wonderful idea, Kimberly," Melanie said. To Elaine, she said, "You've got yourself a real gem here, honeybunch. But there isn't time to involve a printer. We don't even have time to have invitations printed."

"Oh, I could do that for you in no time," Kimberly offered. "Maybe you don't know, but I graduated in computer science at the University. I'm good with computers and computer programs. I can get them to do just about anything. And I've got a part-time job helping out in the computer lab, so I can design and print out the menus and the invitations while I'm tutoring the students."

Melanie could not restrain herself, she gave Kimberly a squeeze. "You are a godsend." To Elaine, she said, "Like I said, honeybunch, you've got yourself a jewel.

"Now remember, hearts are the theme. We could have invitations with borders of small intertwined hearts."

"I can do that," Kimberly said. "How many people are you inviting?"

"Not many. The list is up to forty now. We're keeping this small."

"So if you invite forty, you may get…how many acceptances? Thirty maybe?" Kimberly asked.

Elaine snorted. "Kimberly, you don't know who you are dealing with here. If Melanie invites forty, forty will show. Local society folks have been known to kill each other to get on her guest lists."

Melanie flipped her hair. But what Elaine had said was true. Organizations were always begging Melanie to head up their fund raisers because with her name on the invitations, attendance would be high.

"Now for the cake, Elaine," Melanie said. "I definitely want to use Celeste again. The cakes she made for our wedding were out of this world. But for Scarlett, I thought we could do four round tiers, with white fondant frosting and cascades of red roses made of sugar. What do you think?"

"Simple and traditional is always a wise choice, Melanie," Elaine agreed.

"What do you think, Kimberly?"

"What you have described is perfect, Melanie. You have excellent taste. Has anyone ever told you that?"

I suppressed a snort. Where had I heard that one before?

There were pounding footsteps on the back porch stairs, a door slammed, and a woman marched in through the family parlor, wind-blown and out of breath. "Sorry to be late. What a morning I've had. And what is that infernal racket?" she cried, flashing angry brown eyes upward toward the ceiling. "You can hear that noise all the way out on Market Street."

You could hear Jon's hammering, but distantly. It was not an infernal racket.

I was momentarily taken aback. And angry, as well. Jon and I were giving our time and labor to this project. Was appreciation and understanding too much to expect?

The woman nodded to Elaine, ignored Kimberly,

then raked her chilly eyes over Melanie and me. She discounted me as I was dressed in khakis and a flannel shirt. The only one left was Melanie.

She marched up to Melanie and extended her hand. "I'm Vanessa Holder. You must be my client, Melissa Wilkes."

I bite the insides of my cheeks. Uh oh. This woman had no idea what she was in for. She did not know Melanie? Everyone in town knew who my sister was. And she had called her Melissa?

A brief grimace crossed Melanie's face then disappeared. She accepted the woman's hand. "I am Melanie Wilkes." She emphasized her first name.

"OK," Melanie said briskly. "Since you are late, we don't have much time so let's dispense with the chit-chat. I understand you've worked with the staff here before. Is that true?"

Vanessa's chin shot up. "I am the Museum's preferred party planner. I have planned and executed many weddings and parties here at the mansion. I work with only the best families. I have an excellent working relationship with the staff. And before my wedding planning career consumed all of my time, I volunteered here as a docent for many years. So I know every nook and cranny in this house."

She gave Melanie a look that said: That should satisfy you.

Then she went on, "I am booked up six months in advance so were it not for the groom's unfortunate... ah, altered financial situation, I would not be available to plan your little wedding."

Melanie opened her mouth to say something, thought better of it, and clammed up. What Vanessa had said was true. Without her, Melanie would have to do all of the work herself.

"Now for your part, madam," and Vanessa uttered the title 'madam' as if she had doubts, "I hope you've got a guest list for me so I know how many we're preparing for, and I hope you've got…how long is that racket going to go on? I can't hear myself think. And I've got a splitting headache."

Talk about an attitude. "Since there aren't any guests inside the mansion right now, Vanessa," I said defensively, "this is a good time for us to work on the belvedere. We have to plan our schedule around the tourists. And today we've got plywood to insert in the window openings, and a railing to repair."

Perhaps she did not know that I was one of the restorers. "Tomorrow, we plan to work on the windows at a shop off site. So we won't be here to annoy you with our noise. That is, if you are here."

Vanessa peered at me questioningly. She was about fifty with a cloud of white hair, black eyebrows and lashes, and very dark brown eyes. Her makeup was applied with a heavy hand. She wore a severe tailored black wool suit that was out of style since it had shoulder pads the size of a football player's gear; the kind of suit that was popular when I was a child. The straight black skirt hit her legs mid-calf and made her appear foreshortened.

She gave me another frosty look. "I didn't realize you were associated with this…this repair job. I thought you were a client."

"I am both," I said evenly. "Now if you'll excuse me, I'd better get back upstairs to the belvedere and see if Jon needs any assistance.

"Melanie, you can arrange the tables and the seating however you think best.

"Elaine and Kimberly, your menu sounds wonderful."

Suddenly a tone of hostility had overtaken our fun wedding plans, undoing all of the pleasure of Kimberly's intriguing menu. Vanessa Holder was the sort of person who created havoc wherever she went. I'd known those types before.

I climbed the stairs slowly, my knees still a little sore. And I felt an overwhelming dislike for Vanessa Holder and wondered if she truly had planned many weddings for the mansion. And what kind of docent had she made with that snooty attitude of hers?

She was definitely not a people person. And she seemed to take personal offense at the repairs we were executing in the belvedere.

SIXTEEN

EVERYONE WHO KNOWS ME knows that I am no cook. Neither is Jon. Neither is Melanie. But Cam's hobby is baking cakes. So except for his skills in the baking department, we are all lost souls in the kitchen. Dependent on others to feed us. How helpless is that? The restaurateurs in Wilmington adore us, are always happy to see us coming, and know us by name.

But I do try. And once while traveling I ate a sandwich at Biaggi's Restaurant in Cary that I loved and have learned to duplicate. Hey, anyone can make a sandwich, right?

I use soft, multigrain bread. Mix Miracle Whip Lite with an equal amount of sweet honey mustard, and spread that on the bread. Two or three slices of honey smoked or hickory smoked—your choice—turkey breast from the Fresh Market's deli. And then the secret ingredient: thin slices of soft, fully ripened avocado. Oh, yum.

Now I pulled three such sandwiches out of my cooler and passed one each to Lonnie, Jon, and moi. We were sitting on a bench under a huge magnolia tree in Mrs. Bellamy's garden. I placed my sandwich on the bench between Jon and me and reached into the cooler for a chilled bottle of diet green tea, then filled large paper cups for each of us.

"Welcome to my café," I told Jon and Lonnie. "It's

called Magnolia Gardens. And there is only one item on the menu."

Jon laughed, removed his sandwich from its sandwich baggie, and took a large bite. To Lonnie he said, "That's because there's only one item this lady knows how to make. But it's a real treat, so eat up, my man."

Lonnie laughed at both of us. "You two tickle my funny bone," he said.

Lonnie's scrapes and bruises were on the mend. We weren't talking much about the incident, just proceeding with great caution. Neither were we taking anything for granted. When we arrived on the site, we checked the mansion over carefully. But usually the caretaker was around when we came in at eight in the morning. We'd find him working on some project, or running the vacuum over the first floor carpeting. When he was around, we felt safer.

We ate our sandwiches in silence for a while. Lonnie swallowed the last bite of his and asked, "Got another one of those in that cooler. That's a mighty fine sandwich."

"Does a polar bear like the snow?" I responded. "Of course, I made extras. I know what kind of appetites you men have got." And I handed Lonnie a second.

"Me, too," Jon said. "Thank you kindly, ma'am."

Lonnie had a lunch box of his own, and he withdrew bags of potato chips and handed them around. Naturally I opened my bag *tout de suite*. "Exactly what my hips need," I said.

Jon leaned toward me. "Ashley, you are perfect just the way you are."

Lonnie laughed. "Ashley, don't you know you girls are supposed to have them wide hips? How else are you going to carry our babies? No man is attracted to a woman who's deficient in the booty department. Why do you think we're all so crazy about Queen Latifah? You white girls are so into skinny, you don't know what a real man needs."

Lonnie would have no idea he had touched a raw nerve. If he knew that I had tried to have a baby and had miscarried, he had forgotten. And I most definitely could not blame that failure on skinny hips.

So I did what I always do when I do not want to talk about something: I changed the subject. And Jon, so attuned to me, helped me out.

I told them about our meeting with the uptight wedding planner.

"I know who Vanessa Holder is," Lonnie said. "I know all about the Holders. That family has held a grudge against us Hudsons since before the struggle for emancipation. See, the best builders in Wilmington in those days were the African-American artisans. Some free, some slaves. Our people got the jobs building these fine mansions."

He looked up at the twenty-five foot columns that rose to a paneled ceiling under the piazza's roof. "The white folks who felt like the work should have come to them really raised a ruckus. Trashed a building under construction by blacks. I don't know for sure if the Holders were part of that gang, but the word always was that they were.

"One of the town leaders told the belligerent white carpenters and masons that they were free to go live someplace else anytime they chose. Some did leave. The Holders stayed, and eked out a living somehow."

"But surely Vanessa Holder is not still resentful over

a grievance that happened over a hundred and fifty years ago?" I said.

"Folks can hang onto their grudges a long time," Lonnie said sagely. "Just look at my pa and my uncle Abinah. Those two haven't spoken since before I was born, and that's been over fifty years."

"What is that feud about, Lonnie?" Jon asked.

The sandwiches had disappeared quickly, and I gathered up the baggies and crumpled paper napkins and stowed them in the cooler.

"Dang if I know, Jon," Lonnie replied. "Neither one of them will talk about it." He grinned. "Truth be told: I don't think they remember."

"I've got chocolate chip cookies," I sang.

"Well, what are you waiting for? Pass those bad boys around," Jon said.

Bad boys, indeed. No matter how much food I rejected, I just continued to get rounder and rounder. So what the heck? Might as well enjoy myself. "From my lips to my hips," I said and took a bite.

Lonnie howled. "Don't be starting on the hips again. You keep on climbing those stairs up to that belvedere, Ashley. That'll take care of that cookie you are eating. Better than a stair-step machine any day."

AFTER I HAD LEFT Melanie to work out the wedding details with Vanessa Holder, I had climbed the three long flights of stairs to the belvedere. At that point, Jon and Lonnie did not need my help. I was just in the way. And the belvedere was not really large enough to accommodate more than two people working at once.

I stood on the top step, talked to them as they worked, and stared past them out of the windows. There were church spires and tree tops to admire. To the east of the Bellamy Mansion rose the steeple of St. Paul's Evangelical Lutheran Church, built at the same time as the Bellamy house.

On the west was the First Baptist Church, also constructed during the same period, its tall steeple piercing the sky. Across Market Street, the Carolina Apartment building sat squarely on the corner. The building looked quiet and closed up. No one leaned out of an upper story window. No shooter in sight. Wilmington PD seemed to have the threat of a shooting rampage under control for the time being.

In the distance to the north I spied our tallest building, the new PPD headquarters.

Jon was sheathing the window openings on the south side, shielding us from any threat from the Carolina Apartments. Lonnie was working on constructing a temporary safety railing until we could design and duplicate the original.

THE BELLAMY FAMILY, with the exception of Dr. Bellamy himself, had been members and staunch supporters of the First Presbyterian Church at Third and Orange. And undoubtedly that explained why alcoholic beverages had not been served in their home.

One of the things I love about my hometown is the multitude of historic churches with their heaven-reaching steeples. My own church, St. James Episcopal, is an architectural treasure with its Gothic Revival bell tower.

We would move the sashes to the work shop and repair and paint them there. Then we would get to work repairing the window frames. Wood was rotted out and had to be replaced. After that, I planned to sand and scrape the peeling plaster walls.

When Jon and Lonnie were ready for a lunch break, we had headed down to the garden. For January eighth we were experiencing mild, warm weather. Oh, Wilmington gets its cold snaps, but for the most part our winters are of the shirt-sleeve variety.

So we sat out under an ancient magnolia tree and enjoyed the spring-like day in the restored garden.

As a young woman in the mid-nineteenth century, Eliza Bellamy, nee McIlhenny Harriss, had been an accomplished botanist who derived much pleasure from the garden in her old home. In 1861 when the mansion was finished and the Bellamy family had moved in, Mrs. Bellamy looked forward to planting a new garden here. But the War Between the States started within months of the Bellamys moving into their glorious new home. And on the heels of the naval blockade, Yellow Fever spread to our port city, believed to have been transmitted by sailors on board one of the blockade runners. The Bellamys, and many other families, fled the threat of illness to stay with friends or family in outlying areas that had been spared the pandemic.

Mrs. Bellamy waited four years before she was permitted to return to her home and begin the planning and creation of her garden. But first an ornate iron fence had to be installed around the property. After waiting so long, the garden must have given her great satisfaction and joy.

After Mrs. Bellamy's death in 1907, the garden slowly deteriorated. And during the years when the house was unoccupied, the garden virtually disappeared. But when the restoration of this prize architectural specimen began in 1992, UNCW undertook a research study of the garden. Using historic photographs and personal recollections, a fair idea of how the garden had appeared originally was revealed.

In 1996, the garden was recreated through generous local giving. Now it resembled the original as nearly as possible.

I gazed up onto the piazza and could almost see the large family gathered there, enjoying their garden. At this time of year, there would be pale pink and deep rose camellias blooming against the deep greens and bright reds of holly and pyracantha for them to admire.

Garden pathways paved with white shell materials would invite them to stroll among day lilies and crepe myrtles in spring, the air redolent with heavenly scented flowering magnolias. In the hot summer months there would be roses and oleander, and Cape Jasmine.

Jon's voice drew me back to the present. "Ashley. How about a short walk before we go back to work?"

"What?" I asked. I had traveled to another time and place. And as frequently happens to me when working on a restoration project, I found myself bonding with the family that had once called this place home.

SEVENTEEN

IN JANUARY, THE LIGHT in Wilmington turns to a soft clear yellow that causes the air to shimmer. The famous painter, Claude Howell, who had painted many scenes along the Cape Fear, said that the golden hue of the river tinted the atmosphere.

At lunch on Friday, I looked out the window of The Pilot House restaurant and watched as the elevated section of Memorial Bridge lifted to the top, allowing a large ship to pass through. To the south of us was the Port of Wilmington. And with plans underway, one day we would have a new international deepwater terminal on the Cape Fear at Southport.

Across the table, Melanie was saying to Jackie Hudson, who was seated to my left, "Tell us what happened, Jackie? Ashley and I are so sorry for your troubles. Aren't we, Ashley? Ashley? Earth to Ashley."

I pulled my gaze away from the river. "Oh. Sorry, Jackie. Yes, tell us what's wrong. You and Brian seemed so happy on New Year's Eve."

Just then our server brought tall glasses of iced tea. Like everyone else in the South, Melanie and I had been raised on sweet tea, but being weight conscious had made the switch to unsweetened. How I missed sweet tea!

Jackie said, "I just don't know Brian anymore. He's a changed man ever since Han Cheng came into his life. He's been talking to Han's lawyers in China and he thinks he is going to be taken on as Han's American legal counsel. To hear Brian tell it these days, you'd think he was going to build that new sea terminal all by himself, single-handedly."

Melanie squeezed Jackie's hand. "I'm so sorry, Shug. Brian's always handled my real estate closings. I'd hate to lose him."

Jackie rubbed her hands over her face, then leaned on her elbows. "Brian used to have high standards, Melanie. Everyone knows lawyers are on the short end of the stick when it comes to ethics, but Brian used to be most ethical. That was one of the characteristics that attracted me to him."

"I know what you mean," I said. "I know of this lawyer who calls himself a specialist in environmental law. He represents really big clients all over the state. But what he really does is use his knowledge of environmental law to despoil the environment. He's made a fortune off companies that have raped the land, and violated our air and ground water. Not to mention the wild animals their earth moving equipment has displaced."

Jackie grabbed my hand. "Oh, Ashley, don't get me started on that. My degree is in environmental law and protecting the county against predatory builders has been such an uphill battle. They fell the trees and scrape off the top soil, then sell the top soil back to the homeowners in neat small plastic bags. And what Titan Cement is attempting to do will pollute one of our most unspoiled areas."

"From my perspective, a cement factory nearby will depreciate property values even more than they have already been depreciated by the sub-prime mortgage scandal," Melanie said. "So we are reading from the same page on that subject, Jackie. I always knew those brokers with their 'too good to be true' deals were frauds. And I steered my buyers away from them. Brian did, too."

"That was when Brian was still one of the good guys," Jackie said. "You're both coming to the New Hanover Environmental Commission's fund raiser at the Bellamy next Saturday night, aren't you?" she asked.

"Jon and I bought our tickets ages ago," I said. "We'll be there. We practically live at the Bellamy these days anyhow."

"And you know Cam and I will be there," Melanie said. "Looking forward to it."

"I can't thank you enough for co-chairing this event, Melanie," Jackie said.

Lunch arrived. I was having a cup of seafood bisque with a lettuce wedge. Melanie and Jackie were served spinach salads. We all partook of the scrumptious corn bread. How could anyone resist that?

"I thought the shooting of Brian's uncle in the belvedere would scare people away," Jackie said. "But we've had no cancellations for the party."

"I've noticed that, too," I said. "Museum visits are up. I guess what they say is true: There is no such thing as bad publicity."

"You were telling us about your marital problems," Melanie said. "And Ashley and I are so sorry this is happening to a sweet couple like you and Brian."

Jackie set her fork on her plate and gazed at us squarely. She had beautifully sculpted cheek bones and clear golden brown skin. She was a tall woman with a figure that Aunt Ruby would describe as "spare." But which I referred to as "svelte."

"The marriage is over, girls. Brian has moved out. We have grown so far apart, there is no going back. His ambitions have changed him into someone I don't recognize. He is not the man I married. I'm filing for a divorce."

"Oh, Jackie, I'm so sorry," Melanie said.

"I am, too, Jackie. And Jon will be sad to hear this news," I said. "We'll always remember our fun New Year's Eve with you guys fondly."

Jackie got a dreamy look on her face. "Yes, that was a special night. We managed to put aside our differences and have a good time together, like in the old days."

"Are you planning to keep the house?" Melanie asked. "Or to sell?"

"It's too soon to make a decision, Melanie. But you know if I decide to sell, I'll call you. And we may have to sell in order to divide the property. I'm grateful we did not have children."

"Yes," I murmured, but in my heart I did not agree. If my baby had been born, I would have been happy to raise it alone, husband or no husband.

Jackie went on, "To tell you the truth, in spite of the equitable distribution of marital property laws, Brian is already giving me a hard time about dividing our property fairly. He says I owe him because he paid off my college loans. I tell you, he's just not the same man anymore. He's become so greedy since he took up with Han Cheng. I don't trust the two of them. They bring out the worst in each other. I found some documents that lead me to believe Brian has been transferring funds from the law firm to off-shore accounts. My lawyer has asked a judge to put a freeze on the business accounts so he cannot hide any more cash from me."

"Oh, Jackie, no," I cried.

If Brian was stealing from his wife, he really had changed.

"Tell me, Jackie, did you ever see those bank notes that Brian claims a purchasing agent sold to East River Bank and that were owed by Dr. Bellamy?"

"Never," Jackie said. "But Brian says he has the originals. He told me Citigroup turned over the files to him and they included the original notes."

"Still," I said, "in all the local research on the mansion and how it was built, I've never run across a purchasing agent named Thaddeus Greensleeves. Or any other agent, for that matter. But even Binkie says that doesn't mean the agent did not exist. During the war and the occupation of the mansion, many documents may have been misplaced." Or stolen, I thought.

"I don't understand Candi and Han," Jackie said. "Candi is dying to own an old Southern mansion as if that will somehow move her into society. And all of that poached ivory on their yacht. It's shameful. How can those people look at themselves in the mirror? Ivory trading was banned by the Convention on International Trade in Endangered Species in 1989. By 2020, African elephants will be extinct because they are being slaughtered for their tusks. I pointed this out to Brian; tried to show him what kind of people he was dealing with. He merely shrugged."

Now she was crying, tears running down her face. I

scrunched over and put my arm around her shoulders. Melanie grasped her hand. Poor Jackie.

Jackie squared her shoulders. "I've reported them to the FBI and Interpol. It might take a while, but one of their investigators will be here soon. I'm not sure what they can do to the Chengs unless law enforcement can prove the Chengs were the traders. Probably, they were the recipients of the traders' illegal buys."

"I've already decided to drop Candi Cheng," Melanie said. "This quest of hers to acquire the Bellamy Mansion will ruin me with the local folk. As much as I need a sale, I cannot afford to alienate my client base here in Wilmington. I have my reputation to think of."

"Have you told Candi?" I asked Melanie.

I could just imagine the piercing howls that would come from that whiny woman.

"Not yet. Right now, I'm just avoiding her and not returning her calls. I'm hoping she and Han will get on their Yacht from Hell and sail far away. But I know I may have to confront her soon."

As if on cue, a tiny woman with bright red hair entered the restaurant's dining room. "Ohmygosh! Don't look now, but there she is!"

"Where?" Melanie cried, frantically scanning the room. Then she spotted Candi. "Oh, sugar, where can I hide?"

She grabbed a menu from a passing waiter, opened it wide in front of her face, and hid behind it.

Candi walked right by our table, chattering away in her high-pitched unpleasant voice to Vanessa Holder. They didn't even see Melanie behind the menu. And lord knows both had looked right through me the times we were together, so probably wouldn't recognize me even if they saw me. They were deeply engrossed with each other.

The two women were seated on the far side of the room. To my relief Candi sat with her back to us.

"Let's get out of here," Melanie cried.

"Wait," I said. "She can't see you. And something's going on."

"What do you mean?" Melanie asked, peeping around the menu.

Jackie just looked from one of us to the other, perplexed by our extreme reaction.

"They seem to be quarreling, Melanie," I told her.

Melanie could not resist. She turned around in her chair.

Candi and Vanessa were fighting. Their belligerent voices carried even to our side of the room. Other diners were staring. Candi was practically shrieking in her high-pitched voice. I couldn't make out all of the words, what with the general din of conversation, but I did hear the word "cheat."

"I think she is accusing Vanessa of cheating her," I said.

Vanessa's face grew red and angry. She leaned forward, right in Candi's face. Whatever she was saying was delivered in a venomous tone by the look on her face, but also delivered in a low-pitched volume. I could not hear.

"Candi's accusing Vanessa of cheating?" Melanie asked. "But Candi is the one who recommended Vanessa to me. Come on. Let's get out of here. I want nothing to do with either of them."

Plunking a twenty down on the table, she rose and hurried toward the exit. Jackie and I followed suit, leaving money without being presented with the bill as hurriedly we followed Melanie out of the restaurant.

"Now what was that all about?" I mused out loud when we had reached the safety of the board walk out front. "Vanessa Holder planned a party for Candi. But it seems there is more to that relationship."

"Much more," Melanie said.

"I don't care how many parties Candi Cheng gives," Jackie declared determinedly. "I'm going to destroy her. Just like she is destroying the environment."

EIGHTEEN

"DURING THE CIVIL WAR, Union troops occupied the
Bellamy home," Binkie was saying. The microphone
he spoke into was a small device called a lavaliere
that was pinned to his jacket. A cord had been looped
around his waist, attached to a power pack that was
clipped onto his waist band. I had been hooked up with
a similar device.

Cam was acting as the moderator, asking questions
of a distinguished panel of local historians and preser-
vationists. During the introduction, he had interviewed
the executive director of the museum separately. Now
he invited, "Tell us about those times, Dr. Higgins."

In anticipation of The Bellamy Mansion's one hundred and fiftieth anniversary, Cameron Jordan, as CEO
of Gem Star Productions, was producing a special feature for *Exploring North Carolina*, the PBS show that
aired on PBS stations around the state.

Binkie was in his element, as if he had prepared
for this moment all of his career. His enthusiasm for
the subject of the history of his hometown deflected
whatever nervousness he may have felt.

Aunt Ruby had told me he had been practicing in
front of the mirror for weeks. Plus, had tried on every
bowtie he owned and finally sent her to Belk's to buy
a new one in a vivid red.

"He intends not to be outshined," she had said with a

chuckle. "How I love that man. I am so mighty grateful that we found each other so that we could share a few good years together. My stars, imagine how empty my life would be if I did not know this bliss."

I had teared up when she told me that. As a nurse, Aunt Ruby had been trained to keep her feelings to herself, which made her heartfelt confidences all the more precious.

Our panel was seated in the front formal parlor of the mansion. Two of us sat on an antique deep red Duncan Phyfe sofa. A painting titled "Child with Dog" by Belle Bellamy, the family's oldest daughter, and a most talented painter, hung on the wall behind us.

Binkie looked straight into the camera, not a mite hesitant. "This glorious antebellum mansion, of which Wilmington is justly proud, was under construction in 1859. But it wasn't until early in 1861 that the Bellamy family moved into their residence. Two months later the war began when a Confederate militia attacked federal Fort Sumter. However, it was not the war that drove the Bellamys from their home. Rather, it was old Yellow Jack."

"By old Yellow Jack, you are referring to the Yellow Fever epidemic, are you not, Dr. Higgins?" Cam asked.

"I am," Binkie said. "In the late summer of 1862, the Yellow Fever epidemic hit this city and the results were fatal. Six hundred souls perished of the fever within three months. At that time it was not known that the fever was transmitted by mosquitoes. Sailors aboard a blockade runner, the Kate, brought the fever to Wilmington and this area; mosquitoes did the spreading. Villages further inland were spared. Later the steamers were quarantined before they could sail into port, but by then it was too late for many.

"Thus, Dr. and Mrs. Bellamy bundled their younger children together and off they went to Floral College near Shoe Heel. The two older sons had volunteered for the military. Wagons transported their household belongings and they set up housekeeping in the country. Periodically, they returned to Wilmington to visit their home here. One such visit was on Christmas Eve 1864, just as the Union Navy began their bombardment of Ft. Fisher. They say the roar of cannons carried all the way upriver to Wilmington. And the Bellamys, fearing for their children's safety, fled again to Floral College."

"And what was the fate of this house after Ft. Fisher fell, Dr. Higgins?" Cam asked.

"Confederate forces fled from the advancing Union army," Binkie answered, "burning the cotton and rosin stored at the wharves with the intention of depriving the Union forces of any commodities to confiscate. As a consequence, and to add to the misery, a thick pall of oily smoke hung over the town for days.

"Union troops arrived and requisitioned local homes for their own use. The officers requisitioned the finest houses for themselves. The first general to requisition the Bellamy Mansion was John M. Schofield. After six months, Schofield reassigned the house to General Joseph Hawley, who remained in it for another six months.

"During that year, the Bellamys were barred from their home, except for a brief visit from Mrs. Bellamy to Mrs. Hawley to plead for the restoration of her home.

"Another six months went by during which time Dr. Bellamy sought a presidential pardon for his role as a secessionist. He was advised to do so by General Robert E. Lee who said that particular course of action was necessary if Dr. Bellamy was ever to resume life as he had known it before the war.

"Thus, in August, Dr. Bellamy traveled to Washington, D.C. where he met privately with President Andrew Johnson. After swearing an Oath of Allegiance to the United States Government, he was granted a written pardon, signed by President Johnson, with the oath attached. His lands were then returned to him."

"And so that settled things?" Cam asked.

"Unfortunately, no," Binkie replied. "He was not able to regain possession of this house because, in some bureaucratic snafu, the house had not been registered on the federal government's list of lands assigned to The Freedman's Bureau. In desperation, Dr. Bellamy appealed to the military. Finally, in the fall of 1865, the family was permitted to return to their home. After resettlement, the Bellamy family and their heirs retained ownership of the house for over one hundred years, until 1972 when Bellamy Mansion, Inc. was incorporated by the heirs."

"That is quite a story, Dr. Higgins," Cam said.

"The Civil War era was an extraordinarily complex period in our nation's history," Binkie said.

Cam had brought technicians from the studio. They bustled about out of the camera's range, a steady stream in and out of the house, from their remote van parked at the rear of the house, to the back porch where they had set up technical equipment. A select few people had been permitted to attend the filming, and they were grouped along the sidelines, out of sight. Jon was there, and Melanie. Vanessa Holder had been allowed in for some reason I couldn't fathom. Perhaps because she'd once been a docent here? A few volunteers I'd come to know. I recognized Cam's security officer in the connecting doorway to the front hall.

Cam then addressed another of the historians who went on to talk about the builders of the house, James F. Post and Rufus Bunnell. Inspiration for the design of the house, he said, had come from Miss Belle Bellamy whose sketches of the Clarkson House in Columbia, South Carolina, moved her father and the architects. That the Clarkson House was later burned during Sherman's march to the sea, made her drawings all the more poignant.

A docent was introduced, and continued the tale. "When the house was finally completed, and everything was in its place, the family held a magnificent housewarming party in March of 1861. The dining room in the English basement was filled to capacity with lavish foods. Imagine these colorful rooms filled with guests in their best Victorian finery. And out on the rear piazza, a band entertained them with gay tunes throughout the evening. Miss Ellen Bellamy vows it was 'the grandest party ever given in Wilmington.'"

Cam then turned to me. I had been chosen to discuss the mansion's interior features and decor. Cam formally introduced me as a local historic preservationist and invited me to tell the viewers about the decorations and fixtures.

I had dressed conservatively in a simple gray wool suit with a single strand of pearls and pearl stud earrings. Now I stood and moved to the center of the room so that the cameraman would be able to include the gasolier that was positioned over my head.

"The Bellamy Mansion was the first house in Wilmington to have gas chandeliers," I began my presentation. My voice trembled and I took a deep breath. Get a hold of yourself, Wilkes, I told myself. I looked to Jon for support and he gave me a loving look, plus both thumbs up.

I plowed ahead with my rehearsed speech. "Imagine the novelty of seeing these huge, ornate gasoliers all lit up, when most folks had never seen anything like them. These five-arm gasoliers were manufactured by the firm of Cornelius and Baker in Philadelphia. In the mid-nineteenth century, Cornelius and Baker were the premiere manufacturers of lighting fixtures, having installed lighting in the U.S. Senate and the House of Representatives, the capitol at Columbus, Ohio, the House of Representatives at Nashville, Tennessee, and the gas fittings at City Hall in Baltimore."

Suddenly I was distracted by flashing lights. A man stood inside the front door, snapping pictures, annoying flashes from his camera irritating my eyes like strobe lights. Immediately, Cam's security officer grabbed him and hustled him out the front door. How had he gotten past security and into the mansion, I wondered.

Quickly I composed myself and continued, "These fixtures are made of cast brass. The cornices over the windows are stamped brass over wood. The mirror frames are made of gilded wood and composition. The styles of the three are all similar."

I moved toward the Southeast windows. The cameraman followed, filming the fireplace and the windows on either side. Over the white marble fireplace, a huge mirror was framed in an ornate frame similar in design to the gasolier. The same was true for the elegant cornices.

"The brass was cast into fanciful designs common for that era: flowers, leaves, grapes, cherubs playing musical instruments. The glass globes are frosted, as you can see. In modern times the chandeliers were electrified. They are quite valuable. Recently, a matched pair of gasoliers, not nearly as elaborate or as pretty as these, sold at auction for eighteen-thousand dollars.

"As you can see these adjoining parlors can be closed off from each other by these pocket doors." I demonstrated the sliding doors that were concealed in wall pockets, sliding one out, then returning it again to the recess within the wall.

"The museum is slowly acquiring furniture authentic to the period. Here in the rear parlor, we have another Victorian sofa and this lovely, intricately designed tiered whatnot for bibelots."

I led the cameraman on a tour of the mansion. We crossed the center hall and went into the family parlor and adjoining library. I pointed out the gasoliers, the painted slate mantels.

"The walls are painted the original white. Very avant-garde for the nineteenth century. And very little had been changed in the way of paint colors or wallpaper, so the house was a restorationist's dream come true."

Then we moved back into the center entrance hall again with its huge front door bracketed by side lights and topped with a fan light made of etched glass in a design of grape vines.

The cameraman filmed the staircase. "The carpeting is, of course, not original," I said. "Here on the stairs we have a dark blue runner patterned with gold and red acanthus leaves that is a reproduction of the original carpeting. The baluster is made of burled walnut. The balustrade and hand rail are mahogany. In her memoirs, Ellen Bellamy describes the original velvet stair runner as being held in place by broad silver rods."

The cameraman preceded me up the staircase, otherwise he would have been filming my tush. I continued my narration while following him up the stairs with Cam trailing along behind me.

On the second floor, I pointed out family bedrooms and the bath. Described the sophisticated plumbing system, filling in the missing but recently discovered piece of information that it was Wilfred Hudson and his sons who had installed the ahead-of-its-time plumbing system and the gas pipes.

We made a quick walk around the dimly lit third floor as the rooms here were used mostly for storage.

"And tell us, Ashley, what was the purpose of that loft area at the front of the house?" Cam prompted.

"It was intended for the storage of family trunks, which are now on display."

The camera captured the Victorian-era leather trunks displayed in the loft. Fortunately, the front arched windows shed light on the scene and the crew had set up lights here in the dim hallway.

"But the children quickly appropriated the raised platform for dollhouses and to put on plays," I said.

"One of the smaller trunks is open," Cam said. "Why don't we take a peek inside? Perhaps we'll find some vintage clothing."

I was unaware that the trunks contained anything. But perhaps Cam knew something I did not, and an attempt to capture the realism of the era by packing the trunk with antique clothing had been carried out by one of the crew.

The cameraman mounted a short flight of steps. Cam and I followed. We had to duck our heads because of the low ceiling—Cam in particular because he is quite tall—but soon the camera lights were shining into the open trunk.

I screamed. A baby! A baby covered in blood. Cam was so startled he took a step backward and fell off the platform. But the cameraman, for some reason unable to stop himself, continued to film.

"Cut!" Cam yelled from his fallen position on the floor. "For god's sake, stop shooting!"

My eyes were riveted on the baby. And then I saw it was not a real baby at all, but a doll. A life-size doll. It lay on a bedding of rags. A black baby doll, very old fashioned in appearance. It was made of cloth, and the cloth of its face and arms had been slashed. Sawdust had spilled from the slashes. And the slashes had been painted a vivid blood red.

NINETEEN

"CAM, ARE YOU ALL RIGHT?" I scrambled down the few steps. The cameraman followed me, a bit subdued, no doubt chastened to have been reprimanded by the boss.

"Thank god, we were not going live," Cam said.

Awkwardly, he lifted himself off the floor. His hand went around to the small of his back. "Owww," he cried. "I think I threw out my back."

He was angry, and I've never seen Cam angry before. "Close that damned trunk," he shouted to a crew member who had hurried to his side to assist him with getting to his feet.

The man rushed to the loft, took one look inside the trunk, appeared aghast, then slammed the lid shut.

"OK, let's wrap this up," Cam instructed. "Then I'll get Melanie to drive me to my chiropractor. We were almost finished anyway."

With the camera no longer filming, we moved slowly down the stairs, the crew member and I on either side of Cam, assisting him to descend. The final segment of the show was scheduled to be of the garden. Cam had decided to produce a separate show on the how to's of historic restoration at a later date.

"We'll come back tomorrow and film the garden," Cam told his executive assistant when we reached the first floor. Cam was bent at the waist, unable to stand erect. His security officer rushed forward, and eased him onto a lower step on the staircase.

"Find Melanie for me, will you, Ashley," Cam called.

I found Melanie and Jon on the rear porch, told her what had happened, and she hurried inside to rescue Cam, with Jon and me close behind. Her pale ivory skin had paled even further. She really adores him, I realized, and I felt so grateful. Melanie's paramours had been of the lowlife kind, and she had not loved them, but had forged odd obsessions with them. Now she was in a real relationship and I realized I did not have to worry about her love life anymore.

All we had to do was to keep Cam from tripping over his own feet. He was rather ungainly.

"I HAVE A SURPRISE for you," Jon told me over coffee on Saturday morning after I had spoken at length with Melanie on the phone.

"I love surprises, especially the kind you plan," I replied.

Jon had planned our honeymoon and had kept it a secret until we were in the Escalade, driving away from Wilmington. He had read somewhere that it was a tradition for the groom to plan the honeymoon and for him to keep the destination a surprise from the bride and from everyone else. A custom that dated from tribal days, he explained, when the groom stole the bride away from her tribe and took her to his.

Jon had surprised me with a honeymoon in Pinehurst, home to exotic tribes of golfers. Which had been a glorious, loving experience until we'd gotten the call that Willie had been shot. Willie, happily, had been released from the hospital and seemed to be mending exceptionally well for a man of seventy.

Knowing how Jon loved to plan trips, I asked, "Are we going somewhere? Since Melanie had to cancel the wedding video party she had planned for tonight, we're free all weekend."

"A trip is exactly what I have in mind. There's too much stress associated with this town right now. So we're getting out of Dodge. Heading up to Raleigh for the weekend. And we're going now. Or as soon as you dress and pack."

He was standing at the kitchen window, watching our pesky squirrel consume quantities of the seeds intended for the birds. Jon was engaged in a battle royal with the albino squirrel who ruled our garden. The squirrel was winning.

"There he is again," I said, slipping my arm around Jon's waist and watching as the white squirrel hung by his toes from a twig, stretching so that his hands just reached the seeds. He stuffed them into his mouth greedily.

Jon had become momentarily somber. "You know, I don't have any brothers. Cam is the closest thing I have to a brother. I've been worried about him. What did Melanie say?"

I gave this sweet man a squeeze. "He's doing OK. Two visits to the chiropractor and he's getting his back straightened out. Melanie says he's such a big baby and he's getting bored. He's not a man to be held down easily."

"I can understand that," Jon said. "He's a high energy man."

I wrapped my arms around his neck and kissed his

mouth which tasted faintly of coffee. "I've got my own high energy man."

Outside our window, the squirrel was running off a neighborhood cat.

"When do we have to leave for Raleigh?" I asked.

"Why? What do you have in mind?" He nuzzled my neck.

"Not that," I said, fighting down the desire that was rising from the core of my being.

"I thought we could stop over at Cam and Melanie's lodge on our way out of town. Then you could see him for yourself, and maybe we'd break up the monotony for him."

"Good idea. Now let's get back to my idea," he said, pulling me close. He eyed the wall clock. "Let's see, an hour and a half to Raleigh. How long will it take you to pack?"

"To pack and dress? An hour," I murmured into his ear. "So how much time does that give us for my idea and your idea?"

He resumed nuzzling my neck and untied my robe. "Is an hour enough?"

"No. But I'll take what I can get."

BY NOON WE WERE on the road, heading up I40 to Raleigh.

"OK, now tell me exactly where we are going," I said. "I doubt that I packed the right clothes."

"How could you not have the right clothes?" he asked. "You packed your whole closet." The back of the Escalade was loaded with our luggage. I do tend to pack more than I need.

"It would have helped if you had told me exactly where we are going."

"Do you really want to know?"

"Yes," I replied, sliding my hand along his thigh.

"OK. I know they are way before your time. Mine, too. But I got us tickets to see The Pointer Sisters with the NC Pops tonight."

"Maybe before our time, but remember, Daddy left me his Seventies cassette collection. How do you think I found 'At Last' by Etta James?" "At Last" was our song. They played it at our wedding as our first song to dance to. "And anyway, I love the Pops. And I love William Curry, the conductor. And perhaps the Pointer Sisters were before my time, but I love 'Slow Hand.'"

"Who else do you love?" Jon laughed.

"Oh, a tall handsome fellow named Jon Campbell," I replied.

As we drove past the Burgaw exit, I sang to him.

I've got a man with a slow hand
I've got a lover with an easy touch
I've got somebody who will spend some time
Not come and go in a heated rush
I've got somebody who understands
When it comes to love, I've got a slow hand

Jon rolled his head back and his laughter filled the car and lifted my spirits even higher.

"I'm glad we're getting away. Too much stress at home. And Melanie and Cam have got to take it easy this weekend, so there was really nothing we could do for them. But wasn't it sweet how touched he was that we stopped by to say hello?"

"Cam's a great guy. And we've got all the windows out at the mansion and the plywood inserted, so our timing worked out fine," Jon said.

"But even with his bad back, Cam managed to supervise the filming in the garden yesterday," I said. "So that's wrapped up"

I continued, "At least we didn't have to call the police over a doll. Imagine the dressing down we'd have gotten from Nick and especially that officious Diane Sherwood if we had called the police to report a doll victim. But, lordy, Jon, that doll sure startled me. And when I screamed, Cam jumped back, and then fell off the loft."

"What do you think that was all about?" Jon asked. He was as puzzled as I.

"We've got a nut case hanging around the mansion, that is what I think," I said. "And he's dangerous. But what the significance of a rag doll made to look like a slashed and bleeding black baby is, I'll never know. I've given up trying to understand this situation, but I'll tell you one thing: I'm glad we'll be working at the shop next week."

"For the next two days, we're putting all that behind us," Jon said. "And hope that when we return home, the nut case has moved on."

"Or been caught," I said.

"Better still. Caught."

I lowered my seat back. "I'm taking a snooze." And closed my eyes.

The next thing I knew I was dreaming. A small African-American baby was being stuffed into a trunk. But then the scene shifted, and it was me being stuffed into a trunk. And the lid was being closed. Closing out the light and air.

I awoke with a scream.

"Ashley!" Jon cried in alarm. "What? What?"

I took a deep breathe and blinked my eyes a few times. "Nothing," I said softly. "Just a dream. But oh Jon, it was awful."

He took my hand in his. "We'll talk about it later. Now I need you to help me with the GPS."

WE EXITED INTO Cary not far from the airport. And soon we drove onto the wooded property of the five-star, five-diamond award winning Umstead Hotel. We were arriving just in time for Afternoon Tea.

Inside, the décor was serene, contemporary, but with a distinct Art Deco influence. Our room was elegant and comfortable. After we unpacked, we took a few minutes to browse through the hotel, stopping in the art gallery to admire the works of Scott Upton. His technique consisted of mixing bright acrylic paints with silver and gold leaf so that the paintings were hauntingly reminiscent of nineteenth century landscapes. Then we went into the lounge for a repast of hot sweet tea with dainty sandwiches while a harpist played in the background.

"This reminds me of high tea at the Waldorf, especially the harpist. They always had a harpist at the Waldorf. Mama used to insist on going there when she and Melanie visited me." I'd studied at Parsons School of Design and Mama used to love her visits to me in the Big Apple.

After tea, we took a walk around the grounds. "Trees

are just so beautiful even without leaves," I said. "Their silhouettes against the winter sky are very artistic."

Jon took my hand. "Glad it's not raining. Or worse, snowing."

"We haven't had our annual winter storm yet," I said.

"It'll come before spring. It always does."

"I sure hope it doesn't snow on Scarlett and Ray's wedding day," I said.

"It wouldn't dare."

BACK IN OUR SUITE which was decorated with classic elegance, I said, "There's a deep soaking tub in the bathroom. That's where you'll find me."

"Me, too," Jon said, unbuttoning his shirt.

"Let me do that." I removed his shirt and ran my palms up his chest. Then I buried my face against the warmth of his flesh. "This getaway was such a good idea. So quiet and peaceful. Just pray the phone doesn't ring."

"We'll turn them off."

LATER, AS WE WERE dressing, I said, "Jon, I don't have an appetite for dinner. The tea and sandwiches were enough for a while."

"I'm not hungry either. Why don't I place an order for a late, light supper for after the concert?"

"That's an excellent idea," I said. I kissed his chin. "You're so smart."

He beamed at me, lapping up the praise.

THERE WAS A GOOD Saturday night crowd at Meymandi Hall. And it was fun to listen to the Pops orchestra play a medley from Motown. After an intermission, the two Pointer Sisters, Ruth and Anita, and Ruth's daughter Issa danced out onto the stage.

"Talk about high energy," I said to Jon. "How do they do it? They must be close to sixty." Except for Issa, whom Ruth told us proudly was carrying her granddaughter. She rubbed Issa's belly.

Any discussions of babies made me sad. But quickly the performers' lively tunes and dances lifted me back up. They sang, "He's so shy." And "I'm so excited." Some of the audience left their seats and danced in the aisles.

Jon and I moved out into the side aisle, and danced, too. I just watched the Pointers dance and did what they did. It was impossible not to move with all that wonderful music filling the hall. I simply could not hold my body still.

Finally, at the end, they sang "Jump" and they jumped and jumped. And so did Jon and I.

I felt invigorated when at last the concert was over.

"That was so much fun," I said as we hurried across the street to the parking lot.

BACK IN OUR ROOM, Jon called Room Service and told them we were ready for the supper he had ordered earlier. Soon we had two entrees to share: Ricotta Gnocchi with enoki mushrooms and Shrimp and Grits. Plus a bottle of rich red wine.

We fell asleep in each other's arms and slept late on Sunday. There was a coffee brewer in our room and we made coffee, put on thick white terry bathrobes and went out onto the furnished balcony. The balcony caught the morning sun and the day was mild. There was a three-acre lake to admire, and trees, and wildlife. "This is perfect," I said.

Later, we went down for Sunday brunch at Herons Restaurant.

I looked over the menu. "I can't decide. Listen to this, Jon. Malted bourbon waffle with warm maple syrup, Georgia pecan butter and vine ripened berries. Or, buttermilk pancakes with candied Georgia pecans and blueberry syrup. Forget about dieting. I'd like to have both."

"I'm going for eggs, hash browns, and bacon," Jon said.

"Bacon and eggs? That's so every day."

He shrugged. "That's what I want. I don't get tempted by all that sugary stuff the way you do."

I lifted one shoulder. "How do you think I stay so sweet?"

"Ha!" Jon gasped. "Ashley, you are not easy. You keep a guy on his toes. Every minute. You are the feistiest woman I have ever met."

"Is that right?" I said, not entirely sure if I was pleased.

"Yes. You're feisty and demanding of yourself. And you demand the best of me. And I wouldn't have you any other way."

I smiled. "In that case, I guess I could use some sweetening up." I looked up just as the waiter approached. "I'll have the bourbon waffle," I told him. And then to prove that I could be sweet, I said, "And my darling husband will have the eggs and bacon." Then I added, "Please."

TWENTY

"GOOD AFTERNOON, LADIES. Please do come in. Guy, the butler, will be serving tea in the formal parlor."

Ladies? What ladies? And 'good afternoon'? It was not yet nine o'clock. Who was that speaking? And who could she possibly be speaking to?

I had just entered the rear door of the mansion, which Jon had left propped open because we had our hands full of supplies that we were carrying up to the belvedere. After that, we'd be driving out to Willie's shop to begin work on the windows. I was not aware that anyone else was inside the house, although there were a few cars in the parking lot. I had just assumed some of the staff had come in early and were working in the offices over the gift shop.

A woman's voice was coming from the front of the house. I moved through the hall to see a woman at the front door, holding the door open, and talking to herself.

No, she was talking to someone who was not there. And she seemed to be curtsying. A charade? A charade with only one actor? Practicing for a play?

I coughed. And Kimberly whirled around. Her hand flew to her mouth as her face reddened with embarrassment.

"Ashley! Hi. I was…I was…" She could not finish her sentence.

She was play acting, was what she had been doing. She was pretending to be greeting a group of ladies who had been invited to tea. How strange.

"You're here early," I said, trying to sound bright and chipper, and not at all puzzled. As if people carrying on solitary conversations did not faze me.

"Yeah, uh…"

Kimberly was a country girl, as rough as a cob. She wore the same outfit she'd had on the day we met: jeans, a logo T shirt that must have been a freebee, a shabby denim jacket, faded from washing.

Finally she got her wits about her and blurted, "We're caterin' lunch for a garden club today, and Elaine asked me to make sure the dinin' room was readied. To set things up."

Garden clubs frequently met at the mansion.

"They're havin' a meetin' and we're servin' the lunch," Kimberly said. In her discomposure, she was dropping g's from her words, something she had not done the last time we spoke. She was a university graduate, and during our last conversation her sentences had been correctly and well spoken.

I wanted to put her at ease. So she likes to pretend she's the chatelaine of a mansion. I could understand that. I'd almost found myself doing the same thing, imagining what life had been like in that era, with servants and plenty of money.

"Well, good luck with the luncheon," I said. "We'll be at work upstairs. Give my best to Elaine."

"I'll tell her you said 'hey'," Kimberly said, seemingly relieved that I had not questioned her about her charade. "Elaine and Celeste will be here soon in the van with the sandwiches and the cake. So I'd best ske-daddle on down to the dining room."

Skedaddle? I started up the stairs, my arms loaded. People would never cease to amaze me.

The third floor was gloomier than ever. We had hooked up work lights in the observatory but with the windows there covered with plywood, less light than usual seeped down to the third floor.

I was startled to suddenly come upon a man stand-ing at one of the interior windows that looked into a bedroom. He had his back to me, his face pressed to the glass, his hands bracketing his face to block out any reflection.

"What are you doing?" I asked.

He turned sharply. Even in the dim light, I recog-nized him. He was about forty, tall and gaunt, with straight black hair that fell in his face. He wore a large shirt hanging loose over his pants, which were baggy threadbare khakis. This was the man who had crashed the filming on Thursday with a camera and flash at-tachment. The man who had snapped photos of us as we filmed, and who had been hustled out of the mansion by Cam's security officer.

"I've seen you before," I said. "Who are you? And what are you doing here?"

His chin jerked up. "I have every right to be here. I work for the rental company that supplies this place with party equipment. I've been in and out of this house a hundred times. And I can come and go as I please."

I could hear Jon banging around in the belvedere. Should I shout to him that we had a trespasser?

"Come and go as you please?" I said. "I think not. Only the staff and the volunteers can come and go as they please. There's no rental equipment truck outside. You're not here to pick up or deliver equipment. You're trespassing."

"Oh, don't go getting on your high horse with me. And who are you anyway? Just some sort of carpenter who calls herself a historic preservationist. Hoity toity. As for getting inside, the back door was wide open.

"And I'm not doing any harm. Just taking a look around."

"What are you looking for?" I asked.

He shrugged, then pulled himself up straighter. "Nothing. Just looking at the antiques. I like old furniture."

"Does the staff know you come and go as you please?" I asked.

He did not reply but gave me a narrow eyed look. Then he lumbered toward me in a menacing sort of way, and I backed away toward the stairs to the belvedere.

"Jon!" I shouted.

But with the noise he was making overhead, Jon did not hear me.

"Don't you go making trouble for me, girlie," the man said. "Like I said, I wasn't doing no harm. I'm leaving now and if you know what's good for you, you'll forget you ever saw me." Quickly, he retreated down the stairs.

What had he been doing here? He said he liked antique furniture. Did he think he could carry out one of the antiques?

As I hurried up the stairs, I remembered a piece of information Willie had related. On the morning that he'd been shot, the rental equipment people had been here in the mansion. He had encountered one of them nosing around like this man had been. Was he the same man? And had he played a role in Willie's shooting?

I HURRIED UP THE STAIRS to Jon, dropped the supplies on the floor, and started to shiver. Jon took one look at me and reached out to take me in his arms.

After I told him what had happened, he rushed down the stairs to look for the man. "He was gone," he said when he returned. "I locked the door. The mansion is closed to tours on Monday so there is no reason for the doors to be open. I know the owner of the rental company. I'm calling him. I'm getting that man fired!

ON TUESDAY I LEFT Willie's shop early to go home and change into a nice outfit, red light-weight wool pants and a red cashmere V-neck sweater. I was meeting Melanie for lunch and she can get mighty uppity about being seen with me in public in what she refers to as my "construction wear chic" clothing.

"Cam's at the studio. He's feeling much better." Melanie's voice came from behind Elijah's menu.

She snapped it shut and laid it back on the umbrella table. "Men are such babies when they're sick. And I've been as twitchy as a cat on a porch full of rockers to get out of that house and back to work. So I spent the morning at Wrightsville Beach, looking at properties for Scarlett and Ray. I declare, those two are just letting me run their lives."

"Did you find a house for them?" I asked. "Can you believe this weather? Here it is the middle of January and we're having temps in the seventies."

Riverwalk was busy with strollers. People had literally spilled out of their houses for a walk in the sunshine. Plus, the balmy warm weather had tempted day-trippers to the coast. Business would be brisk today, and that was surely a boon, for in these hard economic times, the tourist business, upon which Wilmington and all of North Carolina was so dependent, had been lagging.

"Global warming," Melanie said referring to our summery temps.

The waiter approached. "I'll have unsweetened iced tea," I told him, then read from the menu, "and for lunch, I'll have …"

"We're not ready to order lunch just yet," Melanie interrupted. "We're expecting two others. We'll wait for them."

"We are?" I asked.

"Unsweetened tea for me, too," Melanie told our waiter.

"Just let me know when you're ready to order," he said, then departed.

I grinned at Melanie. "The service here is always so good."

"Uhmmm," she said, "Now, as I was about to say, we are being joined by Aunt Ruby in a little bit, and then that dreadful Vanessa Holder. I need you all to be with me when I confront her. But first, I asked you to meet me early because I want to discuss something with you privately."

"You didn't tell me they were coming."

"I did say we were going to discuss the wedding plans," Melanie said. "Didn't I?"

"Well, yes, but…"

She raised one eyebrow, impatient with me. "So how could we talk about the wedding without the wedding planner and without Aunt Ruby who has participated in all the decisions?"

"You sure are cranky, Melanie," I said.

"Well, wouldn't you be if you were me? Business is just appalling. I've been selling real estate for twelve years and I've never seen anything this bad. Plus, I've got most of my money tied up in properties that have depreciated so badly they are worth half as much as I paid. And the undeveloped land I'm invested in—well, who knows when I'll be able to develop that."

"But, Melanie, surely the value will come back."

"That's what Faye Brock says. Let's hope you both are right."

"Besides, Cam's got plenty of money," I said, thinking I was comforting her.

"I cannot believe you said that, Ashley Wilkes. It's more than money. Being successful in real estate is part of who I am. That is my identity. Year after year, I've been voted Wilmington's top realtor. They used to say I was so good I could sell ice cubes to Eskimos. Now—well, now I'd count myself lucky to make one sale—just one."

"You will sell one. You'll find the perfect house for Scarlett and Ray, and they will buy it. And they'll come for weekends and holidays, and we'll all be together—one big, happy family. We'll have so much fun."

"Yes," she said thoughtfully. "I can do that." She brightened. "Do you remember that house I rented for the summer a year and a half ago? It was called *Bella Aqua*—so charming the way houses on Wrightsville are given names—anyway, do you remember the big house we stayed in on the south end of the beach?"

"Sure, I remember. How could I forget?" How could

I forget indeed. That had been one of the worst summers of my life.

"Well, it's for sale. What do you think? Do you think Scarlett and Ray would like it?"

"It's certainly spacious. With rooms for all of us. Even Binkie and Aunt Ruby. And the location couldn't be better. Great views of the ocean and the waterway. So, yes. I do think they'll like it."

"Well, do you…uh, do you think maybe the karma might be bad after what happened there?"

I gave that some thought. "You know, Melanie, I have come to believe you can change a house's karma. Look how I've changed mine. And I experienced some horrific tragedies in my house. But now, I've replaced all that with happiness. So, don't let that stop you. Have you emailed them the listing page?"

Melanie bestowed me with a truly radiant smile. "No, but I will. You've been a big help to your worried older sister. Thanks, shug."

I RECALLED KIMBERLY's charade of yesterday morning. "Mel, you are close to Elaine. What has she told you about Kimberly?"

"Oh that poor girl. You know how Elaine is so motherly. She just loves that girl, and has sort of adopted her. And you saw how helpful Kimberly was with the wedding menu. She's been such a big help to Elaine."

"Why is she 'that poor girl'?" I went on to describe the scene I had witnessed yesterday morning when Kimberly had play-acted that the mansion was hers and that she had invited friends to tea. "And when I confronted her, she got so nervous her speech changed. She dropped her g's, and her speech took on a backwoods twang, and she used words like 'skedaddle.'"

"Well, she is from the backwoods. She is from West Virginia. And according to Elaine she's been working hard to lose that mountaineer accent."

"So she's from the mountains? So what? Lots of people are. Doesn't make them 'poor girls.' You know, Melanie, you can be a bit snooty."

Our tea came and I ripped open packets of Sweet 'n Low. No sugar for me.

"I am not snooty," she declared. "Now do you want to hear about Kimberly or not?"

"Yes, tell me."

"You've heard about the big mine disaster they had a few years ago, haven't you?" Melanie asked.

"Yes, of course. Who hasn't? The mine collapsed and some miners were trapped and died. There's been something about it on the news recently. Ohmygosh, Kimberly's from West Virginia. Is she connected to that mine disaster somehow?"

TWENTY-ONE

MELANIE GLANCED AROUND to see if anyone was listening, then leaned forward and said in a hushed voice, "Her father was one of the miners who died when that mine caved in. And it just tore up their family. Her mother had never worked, and did not have any other source of income. And that blasted mine awarded only ten thousand dollars to each of the families. As if a man's life and future earnings amount to only ten thousand dollars! So her mother has only ten thousand dollars to live on for the rest of her life."

"That's what I heard about on the news recently. Someone—I can't remember if it's West Virginia, or the feds—is pushing for more money for the families."

"Don't hold your breath waiting for that to happen. Those mine owners are probably bellied up at the troth, asking for a bailout like every other poorly managed company." Melanie was bitter. As were so many average citizens.

"According to Elaine, Kimberly was in her senior year of high school when it happened. Elaine said that Kimberly and her dad were very close. He didn't have any sons and treated Kimberly like one, taking her everywhere with him. Plus, who was going to pay for her college tuition? Her dad had promised her he could do it as long as he kept on working.

"Anyway, Kimberly applied to UNCW, got a partial

scholarship and moved down here the fall of 2004. Since then, she has worked part-time jobs, taken out student loans, done everything she could to stay in school. And she's a whiz with computers, Elaine says, and graduated at the top of her class."

"Poor Kimberly. No wonder she wears those faded old clothes all the time. Listen, Melanie. I've got an idea. I've got some sweater sets that are too small. I think they shrank in the washing machine, even though they are supposed to be washable. Anyway, do you think Kimberly would be offended if I offered them to her?"

"Good idea. I've got some things I'm not wearing, as well. We'll do it together. Why don't we wait until after the wedding? Then we can take her out to lunch or dinner, and thank her for her work, and give her the clothes at the same time. Maybe even buy some new things to make it seem like we're not just giving her hand-me-downs?"

"That's an excellent idea," I said.

"The idea was yours. And aren't you the sweetest thing, offering to help her? I take a lot of credit for your good instincts, Ashley Wilkes. Remember, I had a hand in raising you. I used to change your diapers when you were a baby." She grinned at me. This subject was an old family joke.

"How many times have I heard that line?" I asked. But I was smiling, too.

"I love you, big sis."

"And I love you, little sis. Are you still trying to diet?"

"Yes." I replied. "But with no luck."

"Well, I'm not surprised. You know diets aren't any

good. They don't work. It's a matter of lifestyle. You've just got to make low-calorie, smaller portions your new lifestyle."

"I'll try to do that," I said. "Jon thinks I'm perfect the way I am, but I'd like to be slimmer."

"Wouldn't we all?" she replied. "But you know, Ashley, you're twenty-six now so you're just filling out. It happens to all of us."

"I'd be delighted to grow some breasts," I said. "I've envied you in that department for years."

"So, it's happening to you now. Give the tight sweaters away. Buy yourself some push-up bras. Be happy about it. You know Jon will be. I know it isn't fair, but breasts are the first thing a man notices about a woman. Even before he sees her face. There have been studies done on the subject. We can go shopping together if you want. What else have I got to do?" she moaned. "It's not like I've got houses to show, or buyers to show them to."

"Speaking of clothes, when do you want to go shopping for our dresses for the wedding? Even though the ceremony will be small and understated, Scarlett will want us in pretty dresses as we walk down the aisle before her."

"Since we're doing the Valentine's theme, I think we should wear red dresses. What do you think?" Melanie asked.

"Sounds good to me. Long or short?"

"I'd say street length. The stores should be full of red dresses right before Valentine's Day. And with this economy, they'll all be on sale. So let's wait until about the first of February, and then hit all the major stores."

Ordinarily, Melanie buys designer clothes. Her wedding dress was made by Vera Wang. And you know that had to cost a fortune. So for her to be shopping sales was something new. "You really are worried about this economy, aren't you?"

"Who isn't? By the way, what are you wearing on Saturday night?"

"Saturday?" I mused aloud. "What's on for Saturday?"

"Ashley! Don't tell you have forgotten. We talked about it just last week. Jackie is holding that fund raiser party for her environmental organization at the Bellamy. I'm the co-chair, remember? Although that sweet girl hasn't asked me to do a thing. Just lend my name to the project."

"Oh, that. Sure, we're going. It's on my calendar," I said. "Jon and I bought tickets so long ago I almost forgot.

"How is Jackie doing?" I asked. "Have you heard from her? How is she surviving the breakup?"

"She's OK, or so she says. She's not the kind to wear her heart on her sleeve. Unless we're talking about animals. I talked to her the other day. She heard about Cam's fall and called to see how he was doing."

I opened my mouth to respond, but she placed her hand on mine to hush me.

"Let me finish. Jackie has contacted some international agency that enforces laws on poaching and the illegal trading of endangered animals. She reported Han and Candi Cheng for owning that ivory we saw on their yacht."

"Get out! She has already reported them to the FBI

and Interpol. Is this law enforcement agency going to take action?"

"She told me they were sending an officer here to Wilmington. She was most apologetic because she knows Candi and Han are my clients. I told her, 'Forget it.' Like Daddy always said: We are judged by the company we keep. And I really don't like having the Chengs for clients. If I can find them some land. Fine. I'll handle the sale. But the truth is, as far as they are concerned, they can take their millions and sail off into the sunset. As desperate as I am, I do have some standards."

I clapped. "And you are not desperate. You are just feeling low, like everyone else. It'll get better. You'll see."

I accepted a second glass of tea. "Are you ladies ready to order?" the waiter asked.

"Thanks, but the rest of our party will be here in a few minutes. We'll wait," Melanie said dismissively.

"Now what did you want to discuss with me?" I asked her.

My stomach growled so loud I thought everyone on the boardwalk could hear it. I glanced toward the restaurant's rear door. When would Aunt Ruby and Vanessa arrive so I could order lunch?

Melanie shredded a pink Sweet 'n Low packet, then added the sweetener to her tea. She fidgeted a little, and then twirled a silky strand of her pretty auburn hair around her finger. A sure sign that something was up.

"OK, why are you procrastinating? What's going on?"

"Well," she said sweetly. And favored me with a dazzling smile. "Shug, I was wondering if you would take over the wedding organizing. You and Aunt Ruby could do it together. Aunt Ruby would be a big help. She's been involved with all the selections."

"But why? Melanie, you know as well as I do that something like that is not my thing. You are the one with the superior organizational skills and the exceptional taste."

Melanie ripped the cover off a straw. "Because that Vanessa Holder is just driving me wild. She is unbelievably rude to me. Keeps calling me Melissa. And the woman has no taste at all." Melanie leaned closer. "Besides, she's skimming. Trying to cheat us."

"Skimming?"

"Yes. Misrepresenting the costs of the vendors by overstating what they are charging and pocketing the difference. That on top of the exorbitant sum she is charging us for her services. I know this because Elaine and I discussed Elaine's bill, and it was far less than the sum Vanessa quoted me."

"Are you sure there was not a misunderstanding? Perhaps Vanessa was thinking of a more expensive selection of foods."

"You were there when Kimberly planned the menu. Oysters and shrimp and mostly veggies. How expensive can that be? Besides, why are you defending Vanessa?" Melanie cried.

She whipped off her over-sized Holly Golightly sunglasses and threw them onto the table top. With narrowed eyes, she glared at me. "I made a few calls to the other vendors and they told me the same story. She is overcharging us!"

TWENTY-TWO

"Jeez, I'm sorry, Mel. I didn't mean to doubt you. So, just demand copies of the bills."

Melanie scooped up her sunglasses and slid them back on. "Apology accepted. And I'll do more than that. She knows I've been distracted by this recession and the poor market. She thought I wouldn't notice. Well, I've been around the block a time or two. She has just picked the wrong person to scam. Her reputation will be in shreds when I get through with her."

"She has picked the wrong person to tangle with," I said. And felt glad it wasn't me.

"I've called each of the vendors and they all gave me the same story. She brings them a lot of business and she told them if they want to continue getting her referrals, they need to prepare two bills. One for the actual costs. A second, inflated one for me. The florist told me, plain and simple, that she told Vanessa to go take a flying you know what."

"Good for her."

"Now what do you say, Ashley? Will you pick up where Vanessa left off and finalize the plans? That way I can fire her sorry butt the second she gets here.

"Look, the selections are mostly made, all you have to do is work out the last details with the vendors. You know, the florist, the musicians, the equipment rental people."

"Are you sure you can't?" What would Jon say when I told him I had this new job. Just this morning, we had been discussing plans to redo my house in town and his house out at Wrightsville Beach to turn both of them into homes for a couple where previously they had been homes for single people.

"I think it's time Scarlett flew down here and planned her own wedding," I said.

"That is surely an option. I couldn't agree more," Melanie said. "But I've got to be relieved of this, somehow. I've been beating the bushes trying to scare up some listings. I am calling every person I've ever sold a house to in the past twelve years. I've got a house to find for Scarlett and Ray. And then there's Candi and Han. If I can find land for them where they can build her dream antebellum-style mansion, I'll do it. Or find an existing house near the water that they can tear down and replace with a big white mansion. But that is the extent of my involvement with them. That is, if they don't get thrown into some international prison for elephant poaching."

And to my amazement, she whipped off her sunglasses again, threw them down, then buried her head in her hands and began to wail, "Oh, the bottom has fallen out of my business."

Melanie does not cry. Melanie never cries. A tiny little suspicious corner of my brain couldn't help but wonder if this was put on. An act to make her seem so pitiful, I'd say yes to the wedding planning job.

But she lifted her face and dabbed at her eyes with a paper napkin. Those were real tears.

"Melanie, darling, are you all right?" Aunt Ruby

asked. We had been so engrossed in our conversation that we had not seen our aunt approach our table.

Aunt Ruby put her arm around Melanie's shoulders. "Melanie, sweetheart, what ever is wrong, we'll fix it. Just dry those pretty eyes and let me see my girl smile.

"Hello, Ashley dear," she said to me.

I pulled out a chair for her and she sat down.

Aunt Ruby always looks immaculate. I have never seen her rumpled or poorly dressed. She had on brown slacks with knife-sharp pleats, a camel-colored sweater set, and a leopard print silk scarf around her neck. Her makeup was applied precisely but with a light touch. And there was not a sign of gray in her light brown hair.

"I'm afraid this is one problem you can't solve, Aunt Ruby," Melanie said but had stopped crying.

I looked at Aunt Ruby and explained, "The dismal real estate market."

"Oh, I've seen worse. It'll come back," Aunt Ruby said, slipping on her readers and studying the menu.

"Aunt Ruby," Melanie began, "would you ask Scarlett to come down here and complete these wedding plans herself. I simply cannot do it any longer. And Ashley's busy with the belvedere restorations."

Aunt Ruby peered at us over the top of her readers. "Now, girls, that is exactly what I wanted to talk to you about. Scarlett called me this morning with wonderful news. She has landed a big role on Broadway! Now, isn't that the best news possible?"

"That's great," I said. Actually, the best news possible would be that she was coming to arrange her wedding, then landing a big Broadway role.

"Of course we're pleased for her," Melanie said, "but this is her wedding. She needs to take charge herself."

"What's the part?" I asked.

"They're reviving *Guys and Dolls* and Scarlett is reprising the role of Adelaide that Vivian Blaine made famous in the original production. But naturally you'd know nothing about that. Before your time. I am so proud of her."

She gave us a bright smile. "I'm so proud of all my girls. And wouldn't your dear mother be pleased? If only she had lived to see this."

We were all silent for a moment.

"I miss Mama so much," I said. "Daddy, too."

"Of course, you do, child."

I looked out over the river, fighting back tears. Melanie had stopped dabbing hers. What a sight we must be.

Aunt Ruby continued, "We'll all fly up there to New York for the opening, sure enough."

"When does it open?" I asked.

"May first. So you can see why she cannot fly here, even for a few days. They are rehearsing seven days a week. Besides, what's wrong with the wedding planner you hired? Isn't she working out?"

And Melanie told Aunt Ruby the story of Vanessa Holder's scam to skim money for herself by having the vendors prepare padded bills for us.

"Why, I declare! Who ever heard of such a thing? I will be sure to tell my church group and my garden club. No one will ever use her services again."

She signaled the waiter and asked for sweet iced tea.

"Over billing us? Why, I know right well Scarlett

and Ray do not have any money problems, but still, to overcharge us! I say let's boot her out, quick as a bunny."

"Aunt Ruby, you are the best," I said.

"OK, y'all, she's coming," Melanie cried in a warning voice.

Vanessa Holder approached our table, pulled out the remaining chair, and joined us with a broad, forced smile. She was dressed in one of her big-shouldered suits, so unbecoming and dated. I had to admit her pure white hair was attractive, but she had drawn on dark red lips and they aged her face.

"Melissa, dear, so nice to see you again." Vanessa was all syrup. "Aren't you a dear to invite me to lunch. I don't get much chance to enjoy myself this way. I'm always so busy making my brides' dreams come true.

"And Mrs. Higgins, how are you, dear?"

"Never better, Miss Holder."

The waiter came up to our table. "Do you need a little more time or are you ladies ready to order?"

"Give us a moment, young man," Aunt Ruby said. "I'll let you know when your services are required."

My mouth had fallen open. Aunt Ruby!

Vanessa turned to the waiter, about to ask for something. Tea, I supposed.

"You won't have time for that," Aunt Ruby told Vanessa.

Vanessa looked unnerved.

"Vanessa," Melanie said. "We are dispensing with your services, as of right now. You can mail me a bill for what you've done so far. Oh, and don't bother to include the vendors' bills. I'll be handling those directly myself." Melanie could be all syrup too when she had to be.

"But...but," Vanessa sputtered. "You can't do that! I've made the arrangements with the Bellamy staff. I've found all of your vendors for you. You...you just can't take over in the middle of my job."

"Oh yes, we can. And we will," Melanie said. "You'll be paid for what you have done so far."

"But...but, who is going to manage the preparations? Have you gone and hired another wedding planner behind my back? Have you?"

Aunt Ruby said pointedly, "Now dear, we've hired no one. I'm simply taking over, is all. My husband is going to help me. Humor an old lady, will you? I have time on my hands these days.

"We are about to order our lunches. So if you will excuse us."

Aunt Ruby arched one eyebrow over her readers. So that is where Melanie had acquired that look. It was a warning signal that one should not go any further.

Vanessa looked at each of us in turn, stunned. "Why, I don't know what to say. I am the Bellamy Mansion's preferred wedding planner. You will be lost without me."

"We know that is not true, Vanessa," Melanie said. "Let's not make this unpleasant. Have a nice afternoon."

Vanessa sat up taller and screwed up her heavily made up face. "You are going to regret this action. I'll see to it. You will be very, very sorry you've insulted me this way. Just mark my words, you will live to regret what you've done."

With that, Vanessa pushed back her chair with a scrape.

"Oh, and for your information," Melanie said sweetly, "my name is Melanie, not Melissa."

Vanessa glared at her. "No. You're name is dead meat!" Then she rose and stormed off the restaurant's deck in a huff. Fire almost leapt from her nostrils.

When I looked back at Aunt Ruby and Melanie, they were laughing.

"Oh my, oh my," Aunt Ruby was saying, one hand over her heart. "I don't know when I've had so much fun."

Melanie coolly raised a hand and signaled to the waiter. "You may take our orders now."

"You know, Melanie, something has just occurred to me," I said. "If Vanessa has been scamming us, do you think she was doing the same to Candi Cheng?"

TWENTY-THREE

THE REST OF THE WEEK passed uneventfully. I could even say peacefully. There were no more frightening incidents; no one fell or tripped or was fired upon. There were no more scary guys lurking around darkened hallways. We spent our days at the shop behind Willie's house, working to rehab the window frames. First we numbered each section, then dismantled each frame. The same for the window panes.

We sanded and repainted, repaired and pieced. Originally, the arched frames had been constructed so exactly, the sections fit together perfectly.

Willie, although recovering nicely, was still too ill to help with the work, but he came out to the shop to watch. And to supervise! He had no problem offering his opinion. And Esther kept us well fed.

Their son, Mason, turned out to be an expert glazier, refitting the glass neatly into the frames. In fact, the shop was his, used for his glazing profession. But he still hoped to get taken on by the new international port when it was built.

A trip to the salvage yard had turned up old glass, not as old as the Bellamy Mansion, but we had to make do. The window panes that been shot out were replaced after Mason cut them to fit.

Aunt Ruby and Binkie seemed to be enjoying finalizing the wedding plans with the vendors and the

Bellamy Mansion staff. Everyone loved Aunt Ruby. And Binkie was well known. Kimberly offered to help every chance she could.

"That Kimberly is a darling girl," Aunt Ruby told me over the phone on Friday evening as she summarized the week's progress. "She is such a hard worker. So eager to please. But I've made it clear to her that her job search comes first."

"How is that going?" I asked.

"She hinted that she had a good opportunity but didn't want to say more for fear of jinxing her chances," Aunt Ruby replied.

"Well, I wish her all the best," I said.

BY SATURDAY EVENING, I was ready to party, and was standing at the door when Melanie and Cam drove up. Cam and Jon had been out on a putting green all afternoon, Cam not yet fit enough to do more with a golf club than putt. Melanie and I had spent the afternoon at the hair stylist. Then back home, I had a bubble bath in my old-fashioned claw-footed bathtub. And had even painted my toenails. My "construction wear chic" outfits were in the laundry hamper!

Cam was forced to park on Market Street east of the Bellamy but that was not a problem. True to our sub-tropical weather zone, the evening was mild and almost warm.

The Bellamy Mansion was ablaze with lights, from basement to attic. What a glorious sight. The electrified gasoliers were all lit up, brilliant light flowing from the tall, floor-to-ceiling windows. One of the windows had been raised so that guests could pass through from the piazza to the formal parlor. It did my heart good to see the old house so lively, with people having such a good time. There had been a sad period in its past when it had stood empty and abandoned, a derelict house, until rescued by the heirs and some concerned citizens.

We stopped at the tent that had been erected in the rear yard. Here, Elaine had set up the wine bar—white wine only for fear of spills of red wine—and a table with trays of chipped ice upon which sat platters of plumb shrimp with cocktail sauce. They were a big hit.

On other tables, the buffet was spread out: grilled boneless chicken breasts, asparagus with hollandaise sauce, a green salad with a selection of salad dressings, caviar topped roasted new potatoes, and slices of Celeste's famous coconut cake and chocolate cake. There was iced tea and water, and on a huge silver tray, a beautiful presentation of chocolate covered strawberries.

At the wine bar, a server offered us a choice of pinot grigio or chardonnay. With our wine glasses in hand, we began to circulate, not quite ready to eat.

Round tables had been set up on the piazza and inside the formal rooms. We made our way slowly, stopping to chat with friends. I spotted Jackie Hudson among a group of guests. She was dressed in a lovely suit in her favorite color, sapphire blue. Most of the women wore suits. Melanie had on one of cream colored light wool. I had on a black cocktail dress with a pink pashmina shawl to cover my arms.

Suddenly, Brian Hudson was at Cam's elbow. I was surprised to see him here. "Melanie, can I steal Cam away for a moment? I have a client with a project we think Cam will be interested in."

"Of course, Brian," Melanie said graciously.

Brian steered Cam over to the balustrade. As soon as they were out of ear shot, Melanie said, "Poor Cam. We can't go anywhere without this happening. Everyone has a project for Cam."

Jon laughed. "That's what comes of marrying a celebrity, Melanie. Now Ashley, she doesn't have to endure that, being married to a nobody like me."

I took a swat at his arm. "You are not a nobody." I stepped up closer to him and murmured in a sultry voice. "You are a somebody—my man. And you look mighty handsome in the dark blue suit. Mighty handsome."

We looked into each others' eyes and shared a private moment. It was if the house and all the people in it had disappeared and we were alone.

"OK, you two, cut that out!" Melanie fussed, but was smiling. She was as happy for me as I was for her.

Jackie joined us. She was fuming. "The nerve of him. I can't believe he is here at my party."

Jon eyed me. Uh oh. We did not want to get trapped in the middle of a marital squabble. This was supposed to be a night of fun with friends.

To my astonishment, when Cam and Brian finished their conversation, Brian returned to our group. He gave Jackie a hug and a kiss on the cheek. "Good turnout, babe."

Jackie pulled back. "I didn't expect to see you here."

Brian grinned. Was he that insensitive? Here he was trying to hide money from her, but acting like they were the best of friends. Or was he just rubbing it in? Hoping to make her mad and thus spoil her success with the turnout. "Would I miss a party thrown by my favorite environmentalist?"

"Are you still representing the Chengs?" Jackie asked.

"Sure," he replied. "Would I cut off my nose to spite my face?"

"Anyone who is a friend of theirs is not a friend of the environment," Jackie declared vehemently.

Brian turned to me. "Hey, Ashley, think we'll all get mowed down by a mad gunman tonight?" He laughed heartily.

What was wrong with him? He used to be a nice guy.

"That is not funny," Jon said angrily. "Your Uncle Willie could have been killed."

Cam moved closer to Melanie in a protective manner. They were staring, speechless.

"Uncle Willie! That man won't give me the time of day," Brian said sourly.

I was incensed. "Plenty of people won't give me the time of day. Doesn't mean I wish for them to be shot."

That must have gotten through to Brian. "I didn't mean for it to sound like that. Sorry. Gallows humor. Since the word is out that the Carolina Apartments is locked up tight, people feel confident to party here at the Bellamy again. Guess I'd better go talk to some folks who will be happy to see me." And he moved off.

I looked at Jackie. She was shaking her head and rolling her eyes. "See what I mean. The money, the greed. It's all gotten to him. He's a changed man."

"He won't handle another closing for me," Melanie

declared. "What kind of project did he propose to you?" she asked Cam.

"Same old, same old. Somebody's got an idea for a TV series. If I bite then Brian will represent the deal. Is he getting hard up? He's pushing too hard for a successful lawyer."

"He's got enough money to try to hide it from me," Jackie said. "Listen, I'm sorry about that. He's just not the man he used to be. And Han Cheng is partly to blame for putting grandiose ideas into his head. Now, I'd better go work the crowd. I've got a lot of people to thank for coming."

And she moved on to one of the tables.

"Let's go check out that buffet," Jon suggested. We went down the stairs, crossed the shell paved path, and into the tent. Elaine was refilling the serving platters.

"Where's Kimberly?" I asked.

"She's taken the tray of strawberries and offering them at the tables," Elaine said. "She's got a lead on a job. What will I do without her?"

"Everything looks delicious," Melanie told Elaine.

Elaine grinned. "It is. I made it myself." She laughed.

"And that is all the recommendation we need," Cam said, heaping his plate with food. Jon was doing the same. Melanie and I took small portions. Definitely, not fair.

We found a table on the piazza at the balustrade, overlooking the garden. "I love this house," I told them. "I can understand why Candi is so nutty over it. Imagine calling some place so grand home."

"I don't know what's up with Candi," Melanie said.

"I found some land to show her but she has not returned my calls. And the Chengs are not here, but then one would not expect them to do so as they are the violators of the earth."

"I thought you were relieved that Candi wasn't calling you any longer," Cam said.

"I am," Melanie responded.

And then some friends stopped by our table to say hello and the topic of the Chengs was dropped.

After dinner, there was light music and a few couples danced on the porch, but not many. Some of the men had gathered in the garden to smoke cigars. Brian Hudson, who loved his cigars, was one of them. From my vantage point I could see him lighting up.

Jon was describing our progress on the belvedere when we all heard a loud cry from the garden below us. We moved to the balustrade and looked down. Someone had fallen. The other men had gathered around him.

With all of the threatening events that had recently occurred in the mansion, my curiosity was peaked. Had someone been attacked? Deliberately harmed?

I left the others and hurried down the stairs, followed the path into the garden to the area where excited voices rose. I squeezed between two men to the center of their circle. One man had his cell phone out and I could hear urgency in his voice.

I looked down at the fallen man. Brian! Brian Hudson was lying stomach down on the grass. His face turned to the side so that I could clearly recognize him. Someone was kneeling beside him, feeling his neck for a pulse.

"I'm a doctor," he said. "He's alive, but his pulse is weak."

From a distance the shrill song of sirens got closer. Within minutes, the paramedics and firemen arrived. The firemen cleared the area around Brian, moving us all back toward the wrought iron fence.

Jackie was there, near Brian. "He's allergic to peanuts," she was telling the paramedics in a frantic voice. She repeated her assertion until they paid attention to her.

I couldn't see what they were doing but when Brian was lifted onto the stretcher, I did see that he wore an oxygen mask on his face. His eyes were closed. He did not move. The paramedics rushed him to the ambulance with Jackie running behind. "I'm going with you," she called.

Then the crowd started to disband. The party atmosphere had ended with Brian's collapse. Very quickly, the house and the yard were empty of people.

Up on the piazza, Elaine and Kimberly were gathering up plates and cutlery.

Jon was coming toward me. I moved to meet him. Then stepped on something soft and squishy. I looked down. A cigar. Brian's cigar. I picked it up, pulled a tissue from my purse, wrapped it up and tucked it into my purse for safekeeping. But safekeeping for whom I did not know. Still, lighting that cigar was the last thing I had seen Brian do.

"Are you all right?" Jon asked. He took my arm and led me from the garden.

"Yes. Just shaken, like everyone else."

"Come on, we're going home. Cam and Melanie are getting the car."

Elaine and Kimberly had reached the bottom of the steps as Jon and I passed by. Their hands were full.

Elaine looked alarmed. "They're saying he ate peanuts," Elaine cried. "There were absolutely no peanuts in the food I prepared. I know better. No peanut oil either!"

TWENTY-FOUR

LATE SUNDAY AFTERNOON, I stood at the kitchen window, tea glass in hand, and watched as Jon filled the birdfeeder with "squirrel-proof" safflower seeds, guaranteed to repel squirrels.

"Those seeds won't make the squirrels sick, will they?" I had asked the evening he brought the new bag home from the store.

"Not supposed to," he replied. "Squirrels just don't like it. They leave it alone. That's what the guy in the wild bird store told me."

"I hope it works," I had said.

On the table I had spread out an early supper: pre-made Caesar salads and bowls of prepared soup that we'd picked up at Fresh Market. The soup was corn chowder with grilled chicken, one of my favorites. When Jon came in from the squirrel battlefield, I would pop the soup bowls into the microwave and voila! a cozy Sunday evening dinner for two.

My kitchen was very old-fashioned and I loved it that way. No granite countertops for me, no sheets of cold stainless steel. I had a large free-standing gas stove, green and camel enamel, that had to date back to the forties. But since I rarely cook, what did it matter that one of the burners didn't work. My cupboards were up too high, large, with glass-paned doors. Now I had a tall husband to reach things for me. The walls were painted a light sunny yellow.

The doorbell rang. Now who would want to shatter the peace of our Sunday afternoon? Hadn't we been put through enough last night?

I went through the back hall to the front reception hall and peered out through the sidelight to the front porch. Groan, groan! Oh, no! Not them again.

I pulled the door open. "Nick. Diane. What can I do for you? It's Sunday. Don't you guys ever get a day off?"

"Crime does not take a holiday on Sunday, Ashley" Diane Sherwood said testily, as if I were a kindergartner.

"A few questions about what happened last night," Nick said coolly, and moved inside before I had a chance to invite him in or deny him entrance. Perhaps because this had once been his home he felt he still had rights.

Diane followed, glowering, her usual sulky self.

How did he feel, I wondered, entering the house that used to be his home? A home he did not value, to be sure—part of a marriage he did not value until it was too late—but nevertheless his home for almost a year.

"We're back in the kitchen," I said, "about to have supper." Not exactly a warm invitation, more like an acceptance that they were here and would stay until it suited them to leave.

Diane remained coldly silent. That was more unnerving than her sarcasm.

In the kitchen I offered them iced tea and was glad when they both declined. I did not ask them to sit at our kitchen table that was set for our meal. It was much too intimate in here.

"Would you prefer to sit in the library?" I asked.

"This is fine," Nick answered for both of them. "We won't be staying long."

Well, that is a relief, I thought. Then wondered, why was a homicide team investigating Brian's collapse? "What about last night?" I asked. "Didn't Brian have an allergic reaction to peanuts? What does his attack have to do with the homicide division?"

I opened the back door and called to Jon. "Sweetheart, can you come in here for a minute."

Jon lifted his face from his task, and in a flash of some higher intelligence, I knew the memory of seeing him there would last for the rest of my life. An imprint of how love and happiness feel. And gratitude. Gratitude that it was he and not Nick who shared my life. All the birds in New Hanover County could starve to death before Nick would put out seed. I was so happy I had a mate who cherished domestic chores just as I did.

When Jon got close, I whispered, "The demonic duo is here."

Jon came in and said hello politely, yet was clearly irritated by the intrusion of our private Sunday afternoon.

Nick crossed his arms tightly over his chest, a clear sign that he would not let down his guard, that he was in his cop's mode. His body language conveyed the message that he did not like being here any better than we liked having him.

So we four stood around the kitchen, each uncomfortable for different reasons. Knowing how they felt, knowing of Diane's personal animosity for me, you'd have thought they'd have found someone else to question. There were many others at the party last night who were witnesses to Brian's collapse.

"As I have previously explained to you, Ashley," Diane said, "how the department conducts its business is not your concern."

"Well, right now you are inside my kitchen, delaying my supper, so that makes it my concern. Why don't you just cut to the chase, say why you are here, ask your questions, and go, so that Jon and I can salvage what is left of our weekend." Without your infernal and pompous lecturing, I wanted to add but did not.

"OK, that's enough!" Nick said, narrowing his eyes and throwing down his arms as if to beat the air. At least he had removed his dark glasses when he entered so I could see his eyes which looked tired. "Just tell us what you saw last night."

Jon moved nearer to me. "We were standing up on the piazza. Brian Hudson and a few other men were smoking cigars in the garden below us. We heard a yell. Later, we saw that Brian had fallen or collapsed. I did not see him collapse. Neither did Ashley. That is all we know."

"Let Ashley speak for herself," Nick said. "Did you see Hudson fall? Did you see what happened before he fell?" He glared at me levelly. He still respected me and my judgment; that I could see.

"No. It's like Jon just said. We did not see him fall. But I was curious …"

"Of course you were," Diane said in her sanctimonious tone. She could not hold her resentment in check any longer.

"If you will let me finish," I said testily. "I was curious so I went down into the garden to see what had happened. Brian was lying face down on the ground. A doctor was kneeling beside him. The doctor—I don't know who he was—said Brian had a pulse, but faint. Someone was calling 911."

"Did you see anything else?" Diane asked.

"No. I don't know if he tripped or was pushed, or if he hit his head. Or what happened. Don't the people at the hospital know? I only saw him on the ground."

"Then what happened?" Diane asked.

"All of a sudden, Jackie was there, and she kept telling the paramedics that Brian was allergic to peanuts. She thought he had ingested peanuts. But Elaine insisted she had not used peanuts or peanut oil in the food she prepared."

"Elaine?" she asked. "Who is Elaine?"

She had to know who Elaine was; she was just trying me.

"Elaine, the caterer," I replied.

Nick nodded. His gaze traveled past me, around the kitchen, taking in the table set for a quiet supper. How must he feel, I wondered again, to revisit his home and his former wife and find he'd been replaced? And not just replaced, but replaced by a better man, someone he knew and admired.

"Who were the men Hudson had been smoking with?" Nick asked.

"I didn't recognize them," I said. "Did you, Jon?"

"I don't know them by name," he replied.

"I thought you knew everyone," Diane said.

I took a moment before saying patiently, "I know a lot of people. I was born and raised here. But we have many new residents. I don't know everyone."

"Same for me," Jon said tersely. "But Jackie would

know who they are. She made up the guest list. Ask her."

"We're talking to everyone," Nick said.

Again, I wondered: You're investigating a case of food allergy?

"Oh, wait a minute," I cried. "I do have something for you."

"What?" Diane asked in a suspicious manner, her eyes scrunched up as she peered at me.

"Just hold on a sec. I'll get it." And I left the kitchen to run up the back stairs to the second floor and our bedroom. The silk clutch bag I had used last night was still on my dresser where I'd left it.

I snatched it up and ran back down the stairs. In the kitchen, I opened the purse and removed the tissue-wrapped cigar. I reached out my hand to give it to Nick but he did not take it.

"What is that?" he asked.

"Brian's cigar. I picked it up off the ground last night after the EMTs took him away."

Diane gave me a belligerent look. "Why did you do that?"

"I don't know. Just an instinct. There might be clues," I said rather lamely.

"That is why we have forensic teams," she said.

I looked at her. Duh? "But the forensic team wasn't there, Diane. Remember?" I said.

She gave me a look of undisguised hatred. "OK. You say the group of men were all smoking cigars. So how do you even know that cigar belonged to Hudson?"

I was seeing red. "I don't know that it did. But... oh, I don't know why, I just I think it is his. Look, I watch those CSI shows on TV just like everyone else.

Check the DNA! See if it was Brian's. Then check it for clues."

Nick had mellowed. "You do have good instincts, Ashley," he said. And Diane's chin went up and gave him a sharp look.

"All right, then, we'll take it," Diane said in her infuriating manner. "But don't unwrap it. Put it in a baggie."

I went to the tile counter. Pulled open a drawer, withdrew a sandwich baggie, and dropped the cigar inside. "Shall I label it for you, too?" I asked with saccharine sweetness.

"No need for sarcasm," Diane responded.

Now Jon crossed his arms over his chest. "You never did explain why homicide is involved with what looks like a food allergy."

Diane regarded Nick. He took his time answering. "Hudson died last night. And with everything that has been happening at the Bellamy Mansion, we are inquiring into his death."

"Oh," I breathed. "Brian's dead?"

"And you think he was murdered?" Jon asked.

"We don't think anything," Nick said. "We are merely observing standard protocol for a death under suspicious circumstances and looking into the details."

"Well, wouldn't the medical examiner know if he died from a peanut allergy?" I said. "What did the ME rule as cause of death?"

Diane narrowed her eyes at me. She hates it when I show signs of intelligence.

"Cause of death has not been determined. Hence, our investigation," Nick said evenly. He put the baggie with the cigar into his pocket.

"I doubt we'll find that Hudson smoked one too many fatal cigars," Diane said and gave a little chuckle.

"Brian's death is not a joke." I was about to explode. Jon grabbed my hand.

"I hate to bring this up right before Jon and I are about to have our supper, but the autopsy would show if he had peanuts in his stomach or not."

Nick responded by changing the subject. "Ashley, I'd feel better if you avoided that mansion for a while." Nick caught himself. "You too, Jon. I don't want something bad happening to you. Either one of you."

"We're working at the shop at Willie's," Jon said. Which wasn't entirely true. This week we'd also be carrying on work in the belvedere.

"Just be careful," Nick said. He paused for a moment, then said to Jon, "Take care of her. I'm holding you responsible."

Jon drew in his breath. Then surprisingly regained his composure. He is a far more patient person than I. "She's in better hands than she's ever been before."

Nick gave him a sober look but did not challenge that assertion.

Chalk one up for my husband!

"DO YOU STILL FEEL LIKE dancing tonight?" Jon asked after a supper that had been spoiled.

"I almost forgot. Does it seem irreverent for us to go dancing when Brian has just died?" I asked. "I do need to get out of here."

"I don't know. He wasn't a close friend."

"From what we've seen of him recently, I don't think we knew him at all," I said.

Jon and I loved to shag. We belonged to a shag club that met once a month.

"I think it will do us good to go out and see our friends," he said.

One of the many things I love about Jon is that he enjoys dancing, just as I do.

As we drove out to the private club on Harbor Island, something occurred to me. "Did you ever call the party rental company and speak to the owner about that spooky guy who was hanging around the mansion?" I thought to ask.

Jon gave me a quick glance, then with eyes on the road ahead, he responded, "With all that has been happening, I forgot to tell you about that. I did speak to the owner and he swore he had no employee who matched that description. His employees are all about twenty years old. He has no one, not even a part timer, who is forty."

"So the guy was lying to me. I think he's the same person Willie saw the morning he was shot. Wonder who he is. And what he is up to."

"We did tell Nick about him," Jon reminded me. "But he didn't seem impressed."

"Well, I am going to report him again." I retrieved my cell phone and called Wilmington PD. Nick wasn't available. The best I could do was leave a message for him on his voice mail with a description of the man and a message that this man had been lurking about the Bellamy property on two occasions that I knew of.

We arrived in the parking lot to the sound of loud beach music. *Down by the Boardwalk* was playing. Jon took my hand and we hurried in the door.

With the room rocking, and people dancing and

laughing, I felt immeasurably better. "This was a good idea. Let's put all of our troubles aside for a few hours and have some fun."

Jon took me in his arms and we danced.

TWENTY-FIVE

THE WEEK FLEW BY AND before I knew it, February was upon us.

"Just two more weeks till the wedding," Melanie said to me over the phone. While we spoke to each other every day, I had not seen her since Jackie's party last Saturday night.

"The market has picked up a bit," she said. "Scarlett and Ray will be here next week and they are very eager to see *Bella Aqua*."

"I think they'll love it, Mel," I said.

"I do, too. I think they'll buy it. They don't have the luxury of time to shop around. There's never enough time for anyone these days. Cam has been extremely busy at the studio, producing a series for a New York company. And I've driven Candi Cheng to every available lot I could find. That woman can say 'no' more often than an old maid virgin."

"Melanie, we haven't even begun to shop for dresses. How about this evening? Want to meet me at Mayfaire? That way we can hit Macy's and Belk's. Or Isabella Grape's at The Forum."

"Good plan. I've got to run home first to feed Spunky and check on him. I'll meet you at six. OK?"

I WAS STANDING in the kitchen, gazing out of the window into our garden, when Jon came in from running an errand. The world outside was greener. Tree limbs were thickening with buds.

"Our albino squirrel has disappeared," I told him. "Your bird seed salesman was right. He does not like this new bird seed. But you know what, I miss that little scoundrel and his crazy antics."

Jon came up next to me and wrapped his arm around my waist. "The birds have disappeared, too," he said, looking out the window with me. "They don't like the new seed any better than the squirrel does."

"So what are you going to do?" I asked, kissing him on the chin.

He indicated a large plastic bag on the kitchen table. "I bought a wild bird mixture with sunflower seeds for the bird feeder. And this wire contraption that holds a cake of squirrel food for the squirrel."

He pulled out a flat wire box and a flat pressed cake made of a mixture of seed and corn kernels. "The cake fits into this holder, and we hang it out near the feeder."

I laughed and laughed. "You are such a softie."

He wagged his eyebrows at me and pulled me close. "Not when I'm around you."

I leaned back in his arms. "I was supposed to go shopping with Melanie this evening. But now you've got me thinking I ought to stay at home."

"Go shopping. I'll be here when you get back. I'm not going anywhere."

I MET MELANIE AT Boca Bay on Eastwood Drive. We like to support locally owned businesses whenever we can. Those are the folks who give back to the community, and in these hard times that was mighty important.

Boca Bay served Tapas, and that meant small portions. Just what I needed. I ordered the Satay: Thai chicken, Thai beef, sesame tuna, portabella, and Thai meatball. Just a taste of each. And of course, I had to have my iced tea.

As usual, my big sister was the best dressed woman in the restaurant. She had changed into jeans after work, but when Melanie wears jeans she looks nothing like other women in jeans. For one thing, she has ultra slim thighs. She had on one of those silky peplum shirts with a swirl design in soft peaches and cinnamons, under a raw silk fitted jacket. And high heels in brown suede. It was a good thing Jon and I had added many large closets when we had restored the lodge for her.

As she shook out a pink packet of Sweet 'n Low, she said, "You will never believe what has happened." Then got busy stirring her tea.

"Don't make me guess. Tell me."

"That Nelda is a wonder. She called Cam just a while ago, and he called me immediately. Wait till you hear this." And she paused dramatically. "Nelda is in love. With her nurse. And she says she is going to marry him."

I felt my eyes widen. "What does Cam think about that? What do you think?"

She smiled at me, beaming. "I think it's a hoot. More power to her. Go for it, I say. A new young husband ought to keep her out of our hair long enough for us to establish our marriage without her interference. And put an end to those melodramatic death bed scenes calculated to get her little boy running back to mama."

"Do you think he's after her money?" I asked and then caught myself. When had I become so old fashioned? Older men marry younger women all of the time. Yet when an older woman marries a younger man, their matrimony is suspect. I did not feel that way about Scarlett marrying Ray. And he was rich and twelve years her junior. I shook my head.

"Who cares!" Melanie declared. "Money? Sex? Love? I am not interested in her motives. Or his. This should keep her occupied for a while. Of course, it won't last. Nelda is a narcissist. He'd have to be a saint to last more than six months. But I'll be happy to get six months with her out of Cam's life."

I nodded my agreement. "You know, there's a saying: What do old men want in a wife? Answer: A nurse and a purse. In this case, she gets a nurse, and he gets a purse. I suppose she'll have a prenupt drawn up, but still he'll be paid handsomely."

Then I considered Cam. "How does Cam feel?"

"Poor baby, he's in shock. But he told her to do whatever makes her happy. Now we can concentrate on our life together."

"How is Cam feeling?"

"He's feeling much better. That chiropractor of his performs miracles." She laughed. "I was thinking of seeing him for this pain in my neck. But now she's gone!" She laughed some more.

"Oh, look, it's Jackie," I said and waved to Jackie Hudson. She had just entered the restaurant accompanied by the environmental lawyer she had been dancing with at Candi Cheng's yacht party.

Jackie was dressed casually, too. Her dark hair was

pulled up in a pony tail, and she had on a sweater with jeans and boots.

"Hi, Jackie!" I called as she drew nearer.

"Ashley. Melanie." She smiled at us, seemed genuinely pleased to see us. "You remember Ron, don't you?"

We all said hello and invited them to join us. There was room at our table for four. "We'd be delighted," she responded. "Is that OK with you?" she asked Ron.

"Would I pass up the chance to be seen with three beautiful ladies?"

But his joviality seemed forced. And on second glance, under Jackie's smile sadness lurked.

"How are you getting along, sweetie?" Melanie asked.

"Oh, Melanie. Ashley. I know Brian and I were getting a divorce, but I never wanted to see him die."

"Well, of course, you didn't, sweetie," Melanie cooed.

"And we can't even give him a proper burial because the police won't release his body," Jackie complained.

"What!" I exclaimed. "After all this time. Why not?"

"They can't establish cause of death, and they are running some tests that have to be sent off to the state lab in Raleigh. Have you ever heard of such a thing?"

"No," I replied.

"I'm glad I bumped into you because I was just going to call you," Jackie told us. "I have news. Brian had never changed his will, so I am his heir." She lifted her gaze heavenward. "There is occasionally justice in this world, thank you, lord."

"That should take care of the money he hid from you," Melanie said.

"I've been going through the papers in his office, and listen, I've got to tell you—and I know you will be relieved to hear this, both of you—there are no papers related to the Bellamy Mansion. Nothing. Not that I could find. No documents from Citigroup about the Bellamy house. No old bank notes. There is not a shred to link Citigroup to a debt owed by the Bellamy museum."

"What?" I cried. "That is good news, but what does this mean?"

"Melanie, I know how you tried to steer Candi away from the Bellamy Mansion. Ron and I think this was just a scheme to see if they could break through any barriers."

Melanie cried, "A scam? Are you telling us that Brian was crooked? That he was perpetuating a scam? I can't believe it. He has handled closings for me for years. I've never detected a trace of larceny in my dealings with him."

"Until recently," I said, meaning until he hooked up with Han Cheng.

"Uh huh," Jackie hummed. "Know what you're thinking, girlfriend. Han Cheng. Well, Ron and I are pulling the rug out from under him, too."

Ron beamed. Ron was an environmental lawyer as was Jackie. He said, "We've got a really big dog from the Fish and Wildlife Commission coming next week. The Coast Guard has been notified that they may be needed to get him on board the yacht if Cheng is resistant. Now this is all hush, hush, so please don't tell."

"We won't," I said.

"Cross my heart," Melanie said.

"I know Candi is your client, Melanie," Jackie said, "but you can't breathe a word of this."

"I won't. This is such a relief to me. She was obsessed with the Bellamy and I would have ruined my reputation in this town had I listened to her and made an offer on it. I've been showing her places reluctantly. Despite how much I need the business, I want to be rid of her. I'd love it if some other realtor would take her off my hands," Melanie moaned. "I've put out the word that I've got a conflict of interest so many realtors have been calling her, but she is just fixated on me."

"She tries to look and act just like Melanie," I explained.

"I noticed," Jackie said, raising her eyebrows. "That dreadful red dye job."

"I can't wait to tell Jon the news about the Bellamy being off the hook," I said.

"Do you suppose there really were no documents from Citigroup or do you think Brain hid the papers somewhere?" Melanie speculated. "Maybe even lent them to Han?"

"I don't know but I think it is time for the Bellamy lawyers to get involved. They ought to be able to clear this up. Just confront Citigroup. That would be my suggestion," I said.

"I agree," Ron said. "I'll make the call. I know just the person to handle this."

"Leave it to Ron," Jackie said. And I wondered if he was merely a friend, or becoming someone important to her.

My cell phone chirped. Removing it from my purse,

I did not recognize the number. I looked up inquiringly at the others.

"Go ahead, take it," Melanie said.

"It's Nick, Ashley. I've got news."

"WHAT DID HE SAY?" Melanie asked when I told the others that I'd just spoken to Nick.

I was hyper with his news. "Listen, you guys. They've just arrested someone for the shooting of Willie Hudson. Nick wanted me to know because of the wedding at the mansion next week. He said that should make us all feel safer about working in the mansion and holding the wedding there."

"Well, who did they arrest?" the three of them asked me.

"Some gun nut. A man who has been on the police radar for some time. An informant said this man had been boasting about what a marksman he was, and how he could go up into a tall building downtown and just pick off the pedestrians below. 'Be like killing ants.' Those were his exact words."

Melanie leaned back and let out a long exhalation. "Well, that is surely good news. And such a relief."

TWENTY-SIX

SUDDENLY THE WEEK OF the wedding was upon us and with it rainy weather. Scarlett and Ray arrived from New York on Sunday evening. Ray's sister Kiki, who was my former Big Apple roommate, flew with them.

Jon and I, Melanie and Cam, Aunt Ruby and Binkie—we all drove out to the airport in the rain to meet them. We took two cars.

The first person we spotted coming through the gangway was Scarlett, her bright auburn hair shining under the overhead lights. Scarlett looks just like Melanie and Mama. Radiant ivory complexion, green eyes, that glossy auburn hair. Scarlett had been a Rockette at Radio City Music Hall before witnessing a mob-related hit on a New York City councilman. The killer had seen her, got her license plate number, and followed her home. With her life in jeopardy, the FBI placed her in the Witness Protection Program, where she remained for six years while they built a solid case against mob boss Blackie Sullivan. Scarlett's testimony was crucial to his conviction.

After that she became a little lost soul. Her career had ended. Her adoptive parents, who were her deceased father's parents, had died. She was our half-sister but Melanie and I had no idea that she existed. She was our mother's secret—a secret Mama took with

her to her grave. But Scarlett knew about us. Our mama
had passed on, gone home to be with the angels. Scarlett
searched, and eventually found Aunt Ruby. And her
two half sisters. Now she had family. And now she was
about to be married.

"Scarlett!" Melanie and I screamed together, waving
and jumping up and down. And then there she was, and
we were all hugging. And Aunt Ruby was crying with
happiness while a proud Binkie patted her back. We
were their 'girls' and they loved us dearly. And Binkie,
who had lived the solitary life of bachelorhood and
scholarship, now had a family of eight if you counted
Kiki. And who could ignore Kiki? And why would
anyone want to?

Ray came right behind Scarlett.

Ray is known as "The Wizard of Wall Street", the
youngest futures trader on the street with his very own
seat on the New York Stock Exchange. Ray is incredibly
handsome! He looks a lot like Kiki. But the features
that make Kiki appear exotic and a bit fearsome make
Ray look irresistible and approachable. His lips are
full; his eyes are dark chocolate brown, almost black,
large and liquid. A girl would like to lose herself in
those eyes. And those arms. He is a big man but not
in an intimidating way, more like in a teddy-bear way.
Cuddly. Very huggable. And I hugged him now, and
we all murmured our welcomes.

Overwhelming Kiki came next. "Hi ya, kid!" she
bellowed at me, and embraced me so fiercely she almost
lifted me off my feet. Kiki is six feet tall and incredibly strong. Jon was laughing, now accustomed to her
ways.

Everyone was talking at once as we streamed into the

luggage claims area, collected their bags, and headed out through the automatic doors.

"I'm so thankful you selected your own wedding gown," Melanie said to Scarlett, eyeing the garment bag Scarlett carried over her arm. "I don't know what I would have done if you'd asked us to do that for you, too."

"Melanie!" Aunt Ruby cried reproachfully.

But Scarlett had not taken offense. "Oh, Melanie, you are so right. Ray and I took advantage of your good nature."

Good nature? I asked myself. Melanie is work. Hard work.

Scarlett continued, "We just wanted a beautiful wedding like you planned for yourself and Ashley. And you are so good at organizing, and have such refined taste, and know all the right people."

Melanie preened. "This is true, Scarlett, don't give it another thought."

I glared at her.

Melanie caught herself. "But in this case, Aunt Ruby did all the work," she told Scarlett. "And she has planned a beautiful wedding for you both. Small and simple just as you requested, yet elegant. The Bellamy Mansion is the perfect backdrop for an intimate, elegant wedding."

Melanie included Ray in her statement. I studied Ray. Were there any residual fiery embers still burning hot for Melanie? Once upon a time, he had been mightily smitten with our Melanie. But now he seemed to have eyes for only Scarlett, just as he had when they met at our wedding.

Loyal Cam just had to brag about Melanie. "Wait until you see the house Melanie has found for you."

"Ocean-front property," Melanie added.

"Let's get the cars," Jon said to Cam. "Y'all wait here." And they dashed off in the rain.

Kiki and Ray rode with Jon and me. Scarlett, Aunt Ruby, and Binkie rode with Cam and Melanie.

"Say, Ashley," Kiki bellowed from the back seat. "D'ya…I guess I'd better start staying 'D'y'all'." Her raucous laughter filled the car. "D'y'all remember that teensy one-bedroom apartment on lower Fifth Avenue that we shared with two other girls back in our Parsons' days?"

Kiki and I had been roommates when we were students at Parsons School of Design in New York City.

"How could I ever forget? A pull-out sofa in the living room for the other two girls. You and I were lucky enough to share the tiny bedroom; two twin beds pushed against the walls and still there was barely space to walk between them. I remember keeping my clothes in my trunk at the foot of the bed because there simply wasn't closet space. And forget about a dresser."

Kiki was trembling with laughter. "I remember that well. We used to kid you and ask you when you were hopping on the train for home."

"Still, I wouldn't trade that experience for anything," I mused aloud. After earning my MFA at Parsons, I'd returned to the South to get a Master's degree in Historic Preservation from the Savannah College of Art and Design. Then I'd come home for good, to take up my profession of old-house restoration.

Ray added, "I remember that little apartment. Jon, the estrogen level in that small space was so high, any man venturing in there was in danger of growing breasts!"

Kiki howled. "No room for men. Scarcely enough room for breasts." Then inquired, "So what's on the agenda for this week? Nobody told me."

"Parties, parties, and more parties," I laughed. "Jon and I have taken off the rest of the week to be with you."

I explained about our restoration project on the belvedere. But I did not breathe a word about Willie's shooting, or Lonnie's fall, or Brian Hudson's mysterious death. We had all agreed we would not discuss the tragic events with our New York relatives.

With the shooter now in custody, there was no need to mention the shooting, and cause everyone to worry, and risk ruining the festivities.

Very quickly we arrived at Nun Street where my house is located. A few doors down was The Verandas Bed and Breakfast where the bridal party would stay. We stopped there so they could check in. We all helped them carry their luggage up the two long flights of stairs, and waited while they got settled in.

Then we all got back in our cars and drove up the street to my house to avoid getting wet, and parked in the porte cochere.

I love my 1860 Queen Anne style house. Jon had helped me to restore it two and a half years ago, early on in our partnership as old house restorers. The exterior is painted a soft gray with white and dark red trim. As with most houses of that era in Wilmington, there are strong Italianate influences in the architecture.

That night we ate in the dining room while raindrops rolled down the windows. It felt cozy and homey. We feasted on Aunt Ruby's Southern fried chicken which she bakes rather than fries—Aunt Ruby is very health conscious—cheesy grits, collard greens, and biscuits. Cam, who bakes to relax—Melanie could not believe her good fortune when she discovered this item on his list of accomplishments—had baked a four layer chocolate cake. And oh! was it ever good. How could I resist a second slice? I could not.

The talk was of the wedding and the parties leading up to the wedding.

"We're having the rehearsal dinner, followed by a party, at the lodge," Melanie announced. "Since the wedding itself will be small, Cam and I wanted all of our friends to meet you, thus the party at our lodge. And especially now that you will be living here part time. I can't wait to show you the house I found for you. I'll pick you up first thing in the morning."

"And you," I said, beaming in Kiki's direction, "you and I have got to schedule some time out for a little session with the Tarot cards. You did bring them, didn't you?"

"Is the Pope Catholic?" Kiki asked, then howled. "Of course, I brought my cards. I never leave home without them."

Melanie eyed Kiki as if she were an alien species from another planet.

I said to Kiki, "I thought we'd take you over to the mansion and show you the work Jon and I are doing to restore the belvedere. How would that be? That'll give the house hunters time to look at the house before lunch."

"Sounds like a plan," Kiki responded. "Cam, how

about y'all slicing me a great big hunk of that incredible chocolate cake?"

"Speaking of plans," Jon asked, "where are you two planning to honeymoon? Ashley and I went to Pinehurst. Didn't golf much but we had a good view of the links from our bedroom window." He grinned wickedly.

"We have to postpone the honeymoon," Ray said. "Scarlett is in rehearsals for her show. And with the madness on Wall Street these days, I'm putting in long hours at my office."

"I'm hoping we can honeymoon right here," Scarlett said. "Out at Wrightsville Beach in our new house. The first chance we get to leave New York."

"The flaw in that plan, Ray," Binkie said, "is that this family will be incapable of leaving you alone. When you are in town, all of us, and I include myself, will want to spend every moment of the day with you."

Ray gave Binkie a big smile. "As long as you leave us the nights to ourselves, that'll work out just fine, Uncle Binkie."

TWENTY-SEVEN

"There's Melanie," I told Jon from my post at our bedroom window. Our bedroom was at the front of the house, overlooking Nun Street. The rain had stopped during the night and the sun shone brightly. I had a clear view down to The Verandas. I watched as Ray and Scarlett got into Melanie's red Mercedes.

"And here comes Kiki. She's going to do a reading for me, and then I thought we'd take her over to the Bellamy and show her our restoration of the belvedere in progress."

Jon finished buttoning his shirt, gave me a quick kiss on the cheek, and told me, "OK, you two can do your voodoo stuff up here. I'll be working on the computer in the library."

We had set up a computer station for him in my red library, but he was running out of space.

"We've got to start some redesign work on our houses soon," I told him.

I followed Jon down the stairs and reached my front door just as Kiki rang the door bell, which does not ring softly or melodiously, but makes a shrill, irritating noise that makes me jump. Still, it is historic and I like the authenticity.

"Hey there, girlfriend." Kiki came in and enfolded me in a gigantic embrace. Kiki is a demonstrative person. You are never in the dark about what Kiki is thinking or how she feels about you or anyone. She is completely unselfconscious.

She was dressed in one of her dramatic, voluminous outfits: a long swirling skirt in dark red, worn with tan boots. A paisley print cape in rich deep colors covered her massive bosom. She flung the cape off and tossed it onto the hall bench.

"Let's get at this. I did a spread first thing this morning and the cards are potent with foreboding, just about giving off sparks. Foretelling danger. What's been happening around this burg? Something's going on. Won't do you any good to prevaricate with me, missy. Fess up. I know something bad has happened. The cards never lie."

"Oh, I give up. Come on back to the kitchen and I'll tell you everything. Let's get a cup of coffee, and we can spread out the cards on my kitchen table. Or we can go upstairs to the bedroom, if you like."

"Where's the hubby? He want in on this?"

I raised my eyebrows. "Surely, you jest. He's a man. He referred to our Tarot card reading as "voodoo'. So what do you think?"

We passed the library door, and Kiki called a hello to Jon whose back was toward us as he hunched over the keyboard, totally immersed in one of his architectural computer programs.

"Hey, Kiki," he called back. Then, "Close the door, will you, Ashley?" he requested.

I blew him a kiss and closed the door gently.

"Kitchen table's fine," Kiki said, and dug into her big carryall bag and brought out the pack of Tarot cards wrapped in a special black cloth on which to spread them. She unwrapped the cards and shook out the cloth over the table while I fixed coffee for us.

I handed her a mug and settled down across the table from her. And told her the whole story.

"And you are holding my brother's wedding in that place?" she asked, eyeing me severely.

"The police have arrested the shooter," I replied defensively.

"What about the tampered railing? Did he do that, too?"

"He may have," I said.

"And what about the lawyer collapsing and dying?" she asked.

"We still don't have an answer to that one. He was seriously allergic to peanuts. That might be the explanation. Elaine swears up and down that there were no peanut ingredients or peanut oil in the food. But that doesn't mean that Brian had not ingested peanuts before coming to the party."

I got up and paced around the kitchen. "Look, Kiki, the man is in jail. He's one of those gun nuts, gone bonkers. You hear about them in the news all of the time. Some guy obsessed over his former wife or girlfriend, going crackers and shooting up a house full of innocent people."

"What this country needs is some sensible gun laws," Kiki said.

"I'm with you there. But the NRA is the most powerful lobby in Washington. And they jump in and shriek about how hunters won't be able to go deer hunting unless they have ownership of AK47s. Well, heck to that, I say. The deer habitat has shrunk to the point there is no woods for them to hide in. You can go out in your backyard and just about feed them out of your hand. How is it sporting to shoot such tame creatures? Be like shooting a neighborhood dog."

"And since when do you need military grade weapons to hunt for a deer?" Kiki asked. "I've got a friend who is a cop and they are scared sugarless. Law enforcement is at the top of the list for those gun nut crazies."

"Right after school children," I said with a grimace.

While we were emoting over our society's inability to control the sale of automatic weapons and assault rifles, Kiki had shuffled the deck of seventy-eight cards and spread them in a fan shape, face down on the table.

"OK, Ashley, you know the drill. Select ten cards, place them face down in their correct positions on the cloth."

And so I did.

Kiki turned over Card One. "We call the first card the Significator because it reflects the situation you find yourself in at the present moment," Kiki explained.

I had heard this all before, but being reminded was helpful. Plus, this was a part of Kiki's presentation and she was a showman.

"And here we have The Three of Cups. How appropriate," she said.

The picture on the card portrayed the wedding of Eros and Psyche. They were standing on a rock, surrounded by water. Psyche was dressed in a bridal gown, flowers in her hair, clutching a bouquet of white lilies. Eros, her groom, was the radiant god of love.

Around them water nymphs danced, each bearing aloft a golden cup.

"Symbolically, the cards are celebrating your marriage, Ashley. This card indicates your present situation. Married and in love."

She went on, "Position two is the Crossing Card, that which generates conflict and obstruction in your life. Turn it over."

I did and we stared at the Chariot. Kiki's expression turned sour. "Conflict and bloodshed. Just as you have described to me."

The chariot, drawn by two horses, each pulling in the opposite direction, was driven by Ares, the god of war.

"He is the image of aggressive instincts. The horses, pulling him in different directions, represent the conflicting animal urges within ourselves. Someone in your sphere is conflicted and filled with animal rage. You will come face to face with that struggle, Ashley. So be on your guard."

"But who, Kiki? I don't know anyone like that."

"Let's continue. The cards may offer a clue as to who this person is. Turn over the third card. Position three is known as the Crowning Card. It hangs over the Significator, in full view, transparent for all to see. And shows what is on the surface and immediately apparent in the seeker's—that is, your—life."

She laughed heartily as I revealed the third card.

"And so we have the Knight of Cups. The Knight symbolizes heady and romantic love. That you and Jon are clearly romantically in love is apparent to all who see you. This love is the crown you wear, thus, the Crowing Card."

We moved onto the fourth card.

Kiki said, "Now we have card four, the Base of the Matter. In other words, what is at the root of your present dilemma."

"Ah oh," Kiki said. "Here we have betrayal and separation. Not you, Ashley, but someone in your sphere. Someone resentful over a betrayal. Someone who has faced separation from what they love."

"Kiki, I can't think of anyone like that. Well, there is Scarlett who was separated from a life she loved when she was in the Witness Protection program. But she is not bitter. Nor resentful. She is grateful for the life she has found."

"It can't be her," Kiki said. "My brother has never been happier. I am thrilled that she is going to be my sister. And now, you and Melanie will be my sisters, too." She gave me a big grin. Kiki adores Melanie, but Kiki is the only person who intimidates Melanie.

"And then we move on to Past Influences. This is what is passing out of your life. In the past, it had been important to you, but now has lost its potency. You have moved on to embrace your new life, and your future."

As I turned over the card, Kiki threw back her head and cackled. "How many times have I told you 'the cards do not lie'? For what could be more on target? Odysseus, the King of Swords."

"What does he represent?" I asked.

"Odysseus is the image of the wanderer," Kiki explained. "He is not rooted at heart, thus not rooted in his relationships with others. Still, he is attractive and dynamic—a leader among men. But he dissociates himself from his feelings. Well, we all know who that is. And why he is appearing as your Past Influence. So say goodbye to Nick, girlfriend, and move on."

"Oh, believe me, I have said goodbye to Nick, Kiki. Isn't that obvious?"

"It is rather obvious that you have embraced your marriage to Jon," she told me. "Aha! Forthcoming Influences. That which is about to manifest itself in the seeker's life."

The illustration showed a beautiful earthy woman with rich flowing brown hair. She was standing in a field of ripening barley. Her dress was woven of plants, and she wore jewels around her neck. And she was very pregnant!

Pregnant? Pregnant? I asked myself.

As if reading my mind, Kiki said, "Now don't go jumping to conclusions. The Empress represents an earthy phase of life. A marriage or a child. But the child may not be a real child, but the birth of a creative idea."

"Well, thanks a lot for dashing my hopes, Kiki. Do you know how much I want a baby?"

She grinned at me. "All in good time, Ashley. You are only twenty-six."

"Almost twenty-seven," I said.

"OK then, old lady of almost twenty-seven. When the time is right, it will happen."

The next card showed a thin wiry man with long black hair.

Kiki stared at me over the cards. "This is not good, Ashley. He is Hermes. The magician. The Trickster. He is deceitful and ambiguous. The patron saint of thieves and liars."

"He looks just like the intruder," I told Kiki.

"What intruder? You didn't tell me about an intruder? You've got to level with me, kid."

"I caught an intruder in the mansion's third floor hallway. He was trespassing."

"You didn't tell me about that. What else have you left out?"

"Nothing. He was lurking around the mansion, peering into the storage rooms. He said he worked for the party equipment rental company, but that was a lie. He threatened me not to tell anyone I had seen him.

"Of course, I told Jon. Jon checked him out. He does not work for the party rental company. We don't know who he is. What do you suppose this means?" I asked my friend.

"This means you have got to be more careful. Lucky for you, you've got me here now to look out for you, same as I taught you New York street smarts when you arrived in New York City, as green as a pea."

She had done that.

Then, finally, we were at the tenth card.

"And at last, the Final Outcome," Kiki said. "But, of course, nothing is ever final. This card represents what you will find in your near future."

With much trepidation, I turned the card over.

"Persephone. The High Priestess. Queen of the Underworld," Kiki said. "I told you I saw disaster. Persephone ate the pomegranate and lost her innocence. She harbors many dark secrets but she does not ever speak of them. She reveals nothing. From her dark world, glimpses of her true self are rarely revealed."

"But who is she?" I asked.

Kiki shrugged massive shoulders. "That is not for me to say. Only you know the answer."

"But I don't know," I pleaded.

TWENTY-EIGHT

"I CAN'T WAIT FOR YOU to see what we've accomplished in the belvedere," I told Kiki as Jon drove us north on Third Street.

"Do they really call it a belvedere?" Kiki asked from the back seat. "Not a cupola or an observatory?"

"Well, technically, a cupola is round. Ours is rectangular in shape. And yes, at times it is referred to as the observatory. As you know, often times there can be more than one name for an architectural feature. Just like the porch is sometimes called the porch. Or the colonnade. Or the portico. Or the piazza."

"I prefer piazza," Kiki said.

"So do I," I agreed. "The name makes me think of soft breezes playing with hanging ferns."

"You are such a romantic. Isn't she, Jon?"

"I love her that way," he said, and gave me a fond glance and a wink. There is no holding back Kiki, that glance said.

At Market Street, we turned east. "And there's the mansion ahead," Kiki said. "I remember this place from your rehearsal dinner. It's so big and white, how can you miss it?"

Jon drove by the Kenan Fountain, continued on Market, then made a quick U-turn around the median, and back to the Bellamy Mansion. He pulled into the parking lot and parked in one of the slots reserved for staff.

"Here we are."

We got out of the Escalade and followed the walkway through the hedge. The sun was warm. The magnolias were lush. Even in winter, the garden was green.

I had planned to check in with the volunteers in the Gift Shop to let them know that we were on the site, and that we would be going inside the mansion.

"Wonder what's going on," I speculated. The volunteers and the staff were assembled outside.

The group of about seven had gathered in the rear yard. They had formed a tight knot, surrounding something or someone. They were all talking at once, all chattering excitedly.

Jon, Kiki, and I drew nearer.

"What's going on?" I asked one of the volunteers I knew by face but not by name.

"The police are on their way," she said loudly. "It's just awful. How could this happen?"

And indeed, sirens could be heard coming from a distance. Their sound had become all too familiar. It was as if emergency sirens had become the background music of my life.

"But what happened?" Jon shouted over the raised voices.

Kiki had a strange look on her face, fatalistic, expecting the worst.

"The site manager came out to drain the cistern," the volunteer explained. "You know how it fills up after a few rainy days."

The cistern had once been a functioning source of non-drinking water for the house. Rain water was caught by the gutters and downspouts, and drained underground into the cistern.

The volunteer went on, "When he dragged the stone slab off the opening, and reached in to pull up the pump, he saw a body floating in the water. The cistern is quite full after these rainy days. And somehow, someone fell in and drowned. He came running inside and called 911. How could someone fall into the cistern?"

And if they fell in, I asked myself, how did they pull the stone slab back over the opening?

Fire trucks arrived and in seconds the rear yard was overrun with big, burly firemen who looked like they spent every free moment lifting weights.

"Get back, folks! Get back!" the man the others called Captain was shouting. "Y'all wait for us over there." And he motioned to the gift shop.

"Guess we'd better go back inside," the volunteer said. "You can come in and wait with us, Ashley."

"OK," I said. "We're coming."

But I had other ideas.

"Come on," I said to Jon and Kiki, and sidestepped around the advancing crowd. I made by way toward the open basement door of the mansion.

Jon and Kiki caught up. "Where are we going?" Jon asked.

Kiki was strangely silent.

"Shush," I said. "Walk slowly. Just act normal, like we have every right to go inside."

I led us down the steps and across the sheltered area way under the porch. One of the tarps lay in a heap at the side of the door. Casually, we strolled through the open doorway.

"We'll go upstairs," I said.

"I don't remember seeing this when I was here," Kiki said. "Wow! Talk about giving off vibes. This area sure does."

I led us through the former kitchen, to the stairs. We took the stairs to the first floor which was unoccupied, everyone being outside.

"We'll be able to see everything from the back porch," I said.

We walked through the hallway without anyone challenging us. Stepping out onto the back porch, we moved to the louvered panels that sheltered one side of the porch.

"Good idea," Jon said, and parted the louvers just wide enough for us to see out but hopefully not be seen by the firemen. We had a clear view down into the rear yard.

The firemen were leaning over the open cistern. Immediately, they were joined by uniformed police officers. The ambulance pulled into the parking lot, sirens warbling, and parked right at the opening in the hedge. The doors flew open and they jumped out, then dragged equipment out of the rear.

"Oh, look, there's Nick."

"Where? Where?" Kiki asked.

I pointed.

"And Diane Sherwood," Jon said.

The first responders and the homicide detectives consulted with each other. Then the group parted, making way for one of the firemen who had a coil of thick rope looped over his arm.

"He's going in," Jon said.

We now had a clear view of the open cistern.

"I can see something," I said. "Can you?"

"I see red hair!" Kiki gasped.

Red hair spread on the surface of the water. The cistern was not wide in circumference. The body was floating upright.

Kiki gasped again. "That hair is just like Melanie's. That can't be Melanie down there!" She turned to me, eyes wide, full of fear.

"Oh, no," Jon said, shaking his head.

"No. No. That can't be Melanie," I said. "Melanie is with Ray and Scarlett. They're out at Wrightsville Beach. I saw them leave."

Kiki heaved a huge sigh of relief. "You're right. I saw them leave, too. It's just that…that's her hair color. How many people have hair that color?"

I could think of only one. Jon and I exchanged knowing glances before turning back to watch the drama below us.

The fireman lowered himself into the water. I was able to see his head but I could not see exactly what he was doing. Tying the rope around the body, I assumed.

In a minute, he was motioning to the other firemen. Then they were hauling the body out of the water. It did not take much effort; the body was very small. The body of a woman with a child's stature.

They laid her out on the sunny concrete.

"It's her," I said. "It's Candi Cheng."

TWENTY-NINE

THE NEXT MORNING, after a sleepless night during which I tossed and turned and saw visions of Candi Cheng, sopping wet and dead, laid out on the sunny concrete, Jon called to me from the library. "Ashley, come in here quick!"

Quick? I couldn't move quickly if my life depended on it. I was in a fog. I picked up my coffee mug and poked along like a zombie into the library.

"What?" I grumbled.

Jon was standing before the flat screen television we had attached to the wall. He had slept soundly while I had tossed and turned. How does he do it?

"There's news," he cried. "This guy is saying Candi Cheng's drowning was an accident."

A local TV journalist was interviewing a man.

"Who is he?" I asked.

"Local security officer. Ssshhh and listen."

A balding man of about fifty was saying, "I have a small security company. I'm hired to handle special situations. The Bellamy Museum folks hired me to figure out why their alarm kept going off during the night. No break-ins could be discovered, although there were items pilfered. The alarm system technicians verified the alarm was working properly."

The interviewer started to interrupt as they so often do, but the man forged ahead. "So acting on a hunch that someone must be hiding inside the mansion until after hours when the house was locked up and the alarm set, I began staking out the place at night."

"And what happened when you were on your stake out last night?" the interviewer asked.

"Sure 'nuff, I saw a light dancing around inside the mansion, coming from that first floor formal room. I called the police and they moved in quietly. See, they had been alerted about the problem. So me and some uniforms drew our guns, and we climbed up those big front porch steps, e-e-asy as you please, real quiet like.

"I had the key card in my hand. I slid it into the slot. That released the lock on the front door. But it didn't set off the alarm. Not yet. Not until we were in position. We kicked that door open and stormed in there. Took the intruder completely by surprise."

The interviewer was on the edge of her chair. "What was he doing?"

The security officer beamed. He was experiencing his fifteen minutes of fame and loving every minute. "The guy was up on a step ladder. Just about fell off when he saw us. Had a big wire cutter and was about to cut down the chandelier. You know, that big brass chandelier that hangs in the parlor. The one that used to burn gas."

"The gasolier?"

"Yes, ma'am, that's the one. The chandelier that they showed on that TV show they did on the mansion. The one that historic preservationist said was worth eighteen thousand dollars."

"He was trying to steal a chandelier?" the interviewer asked.

"Yes, ma'am. He owned up to everything. Seemed real proud of what he had gotten away with. A thin, wiry guy of about forty. Couldn't help bragging about how he'd fooled folks."

The security officer was so excited, he couldn't sit still or hold his hands still. He fidgeted and waved his hands around in the air as he went on.

"See, this is what he'd do. He'd go into the mansion like a tourist, take one of those self-guided tours so he'd have the key card and be on his own. Then he'd take a picture of an antique. Post it on eBay and when he got a buyer, he'd go into the mansion and hide until nightfall. Then he'd come out, steal the piece, leave. But he'd set off the alarm. But what did he care? He was long gone by the time the police arrived. And it would look like a false alarm."

The interviewer smiled at him encouragingly. "Until you figured out what was happening."

The security officer beamed again. "Hard to fool old Jake. I've been in this business since I was a kid. Seen it all."

The interviewer said importantly. "But you made another discovery while you were surveilling the Bellamy Mansion last night, didn't you? Tell us about what you discovered."

"Well, you know, they done found that lady drowned in that cistern. And they are trying to figure out if it was murder or an accident. Well, based on what I saw, it was an accident. What that woman was during there at night, I can't imagine. But she must of fell into that cistern."

"Tell us why you believe this, Jake. What you saw," the interviewer invited.

The security officer parsed his words dramatically. "I was creeping around at the back of the mansion, keeping a low profile. I noticed that big stone slab that covers the cistern was kinda half off the hole. I thought to myself, that's not safe. So I eased the thing back in place. I had to be real quiet about it so the perp in the house wouldn't hear me. But I got that cistern covered up."

"And you did not look down into the cistern as you replaced the slab, did you?"

"No, ma'am, couldn't risk shining a light. I had no idea that lady was down there. Otherwise, I'd' a radioed for help. Maybe saved her. I feel real bad."

JON CLICKED OFF the TV. "So she fell in. I'm like the security guard. What in the world was she doing there at night? And how did the cover get ajar? If that had happened before the museum closed, someone would have noticed."

I thought about what he was saying, not easy to do in my sleep-deprived haze. "According to Melanie she was obsessed with that mansion. Maybe she imagined herself living there, transformed into a Southern belle. You know, she had her hair colored to look like Melanie. Maybe she'd start wearing hoop skirts. Who knows? She was strange. So she drove into town at night, visited the mansion, maybe sat on the porch? Pretended it was hers?"

"And you think she tripped and fell into the cistern?"

"Sure. Maybe she hit her head, or something." I yawned.

"Sweetheart, why don't you go back to bed? I'll go

over to Willie's shop. Do some work on the windows. So I won't disturb you."

"Oh, I'd love to. I'm so sleepy I can't hold my eyes open."

"Don't even try. Go ahead. Get some rest. I'll turn off the coffee pot and lock up." He gave me a kiss. "See you later."

I set down my coffee cup and dragged myself up the stairs. Drew the shades, took off my robe, and slipped between the sheets.

I think I fell asleep as soon as my head hit the pillow.

I was sleeping hard when a shrill, jangling noise drew me into wakefulness. That blamed door bell!

"NICK, WHAT ARE YOU doing here?" I opened the door and let him in. Nick was showing up at my house much too often.

He took in my tousled hair, my robe over my night-gown. He got a dreamy expression on his face. "I always loved your morning look," he said huskily.

I took a step back. "This is not a good idea, Nick. It's over, don't you get it? Jon's not here. And you shouldn't be here."

Nick studied my face intently. He heard. And he knew I was right. Swiftly, he assumed his cop's mantle. "Sorry, that was out of line. I'm here on police business."

"OK," I replied. "Then you wait right here while I go upstairs and dress. I'll only be a minute."

"Be all right if I go back to the kitchen and put on some coffee? It's been a rough morning. Surely coffee is not inappropriate, is it?"

"Sure," I said. "Make yourself at home." It used to yours, I thought. It's not like you don't know that I keep the coffee beans in the freezer. Or what I look like first thing in the morning.

HAIR COMBED, dressed in jeans and a tee shirt, I joined him in the kitchen five minutes later. "So, what's going on?" I asked him as he handed me a cup of coffee.

"Sit down, Ashley, I've got something important to tell you. And this won't be easy."

I cried out in alarm. "Wait a minute, you're not here to tell me that something has happened to someone I love, are you? Jon? Is Jon all right? Aunt Ruby or Binkie? Oh no, Melanie. Something happened to Melanie."

"No, no, Ashley. I'm sorry I scared you." He took a step toward me and wrapped his arms around me. "It's OK, baby. Everyone you love is OK."

My eyes burned with hot tears of fear. For a second I leaned on him. Everyone I loved was OK.

I used to love this man, I thought. His strong arms were familiar. His firm body was familiar. His scent was familiar. For a second, I yielded.

And then I caught myself. The man inside Nick's body was a stranger to me. I had never really known him, not even when I was married to him. He was so utterly complex. So unknown, even to himself. And as Kiki had seen in the cards: a man not rooted at heart. Not rooted in his relationships with others. And while he was attractive and dynamic—a leader among men—he was able to dissociate himself from his feelings too easily. Or too late. For now it seemed he had genuine feelings for me.

I moved away, pulled out a chair, and sat down. He poured himself a cup of coffee and settled at the opposite side of the table.

"All right, Nick, what is this all about?"

He regarded me with beautiful hazel eyes. "First, I have got to ask you a question. I noticed that you were limping a couple of weeks ago. What was that about? How did you injure your leg?"

I shrugged, feeling maybe a little guilty. Jon and I had never reported that near hit and run to the police. "A car going a little too fast on Front Street, that's all," I said. "Jon and I had to jump clear of it. I fell on the sidewalk and hurt my knee."

"A car going a little too fast?" he asked. "Or a car deliberately trying to run you down?"

I heaved a big sigh. "That may be true. The driver didn't try to stop," I confessed. "Or slow down."

"We have a witness," Nick said. "The driver sped up, aimed right for you."

"A witness?" I asked, my mouth dry. I took a sip of the coffee.

"Yes, a witness." He looked at me searchingly. "Why didn't you report this?"

I hesitated.

"Tell me honestly, Ashley."

"OK. If you really want to know. It was because you were in our lives much too much. You were always turning up. And my marriage to Jon is so new. I didn't want any interference from you. So there. You asked. That is the answer."

Nick looked hurt for a second. Then steely. "I was showing up because I was doing my job. People have been injured, and one died, under suspicious circumstances. It is my job to investigate. It is my job to protect you. Even from yourself and your poor decisions."

"What poor decisions!" I exclaimed. Here we go again. Blame me, the victim. "Restoring the belvedere at the Bellamy Mansion? That was a poor decision? Well, you should be the first to understand. Because that is *my* job. And like you, I was just doing *my* job!"

"OK. OK. Cool down. This isn't going like I planned."

"It never does," I said with finality.

Then I remembered that he had a reason for being here.

"I didn't come here to quarrel with you, Ashley. I came here to apologize."

"For what?" I asked.

Nick took a moment, framing his response. "As I said there was a witness to your near hit and run. He got the car's plate number, and reported what he had seen to us. He described you and Jon. And he said he watched as Jon carried you into a nearby house."

"Binkie's house," I said.

Nick nodded, then continued, "I assumed so from the location. The witness said he saw that you were getting help, so he did not offer assistance."

"I assume you traced the plate number then. Whose car was it?"

Nick blew out his breath. "The car belongs to Diane."

"Diane Sherwood? Detective Diane Sherwood? Tried to run us down?" I shook my head, my mouth hanging open, my eyes wide. "I can't believe that."

"Internal Affairs investigated. She admitted it.

She said she just lost it when she saw you. She hadn't planned to aim her car at you, but when she saw you out there in the street, she just lost it. Her jealousy and rage took over."

"I don't believe this," I repeated.

"She's been suspended," Nick said. "She has to see a shrink. She's ruined her career. Might get desk duty, but I doubt the chief will take her back under any circumstances. She's a loose cannon. And you are free to press charges if you want to."

"But why did she do it, Nick? Why? Does she really hate me that much?"

"I'd say this is partly my fault. I never meant to lead her on. She misinterpreted my friendship for something more. Thought it meant more. And she saw you as her adversary. As someone who was preventing me from moving on and getting involved with her."

"And was she right?" I asked.

"Yes," was all he said.

"I'm sorry, Nick."

"Me, too, Ashley." He rose. I walked him to the door. "Stay away from that mansion as much as possible," he said. "Candi Cheng did not fall into the cistern. She was murdered."

"What?" I exclaimed. "How do you know?"

"No water in her lungs. She was dead before she was dumped in. Cause of death was blunt force trauma to the head. Someone hit her. Repeatedly. And hit her hard."

THIRTY

"HE LEFT! HE JUST PLAIN LEFT. Sailed out of port in the dead of night. Like some eighteenth-century pirate." Jackie Hudson was livid.

On Thursday, we were holding a bridal shower for Scarlett at the Wilmington Tea Room on Water Street that overlooked the Cape Fear River. The air was a bit nippy and breezy, not warm enough to sit out on their deck that adjoined the River Walk. But it was sunny, and sunshine shone in warmly through the multi-paned French doors.

"Who left?" Scarlett asked. She turned to me. "Who is she talking about?"

All the girls were talking at once. There was Melanie and her good friend realtor Faye Brock; Kiki of course; Aunt Ruby who at seventy-four was still a girly girl; Elaine McDuff; Scarlett and I. And Jackie Hudson who had brought Esther, Brian's aunt and Willie's wife to the shower.

Jackie's phone call last night, asking for permission to bring Esther Hudson to the shower had completely surprised me. But I quickly told her that Esther Hudson was more than welcome, welcomed anywhere she went, a delightful lady who was loved and admired by everyone who knew her.

"It has taken Brian's death," Jackie had told me, "to bring the Hudson family to their senses. Uncle Willie called me to ask about the funeral plans. And I had to tell him that they were on hold. The police were not releasing his body for burial just yet."

I had commiserated with her about the delay, and wondered to myself what was going on. Why were they holding him?

So we had all turned up at the bridal shower, dressed formally for high tea in dresses and high heels, stopping short of hats and gloves. We were colorful and perfumed and the tea ceremony was a ladylike event. Or supposed to be.

But no ceremonious event could deter the talk of Candi Cheng's drowning which had been ruled a homicide. And there was nothing ladylike about the talk of her murder.

"Whom are we discussing, child?" Aunt Ruby asked Jackie. "Who sailed away like a pirate?"

Jackie was so outraged she was practically ranting. "Han! Han Cheng! I told y'all that I had arranged for a top law enforcement officer from the Fish and Wildlife Service to come to make an inspection of the contraband aboard Han's yacht. Fish and Wildlife has jurisdiction over imports when they involve endangered species. And because there is an international treaty against the harvesting…

"Harvesting! That is what they call it. Can you imagine? Like they were talking about vegetables. More like murder, I'd say.

"Anyway, there is an international treaty against the trade in ivory because the elephants have become an endangered species. So the F&W has jurisdiction. The agent told us that since Han had sailed into U.S. waters, he had the authority to search the yacht and to fine and perhaps even jail Han for trading in ivory."

"Oh, it was dreadful," Melanie said, and went on to tell everyone about how the ivory had been molded into bathroom fixtures.

"Oh, no," the girls gasped. "How awful."

"I adore elephants," someone said.

On the table before us, lay a lovely blue and white tea service: squat teapot, a sugar bowl with sugar cubes and silver tongs, a cream pitcher, dainty blue and white teacups and saucers. But no one was touching the tea. Everyone had paused to listen to Jackie.

"Ron and I met the inspector at the airport early this morning. We drove him out to the Wrightsville Marina. Han and his crew and the yacht had simply vanished. Hoisted anchor during the night and sailed away."

"But what about Candi?" I exclaimed. "Are you saying he sailed away and left Candi's body behind in the morgue?"

"That is precisely what I am saying, Ashley," Jackie declared vehemently.

"Ohmygosh! Do you think he killed her, and that is why he fled?" I asked.

"I would not put murder past that man," Jackie said. "And I do think he is running from the law. Somehow he got wind that the wildlife agent was coming to inspect his yacht."

Esther stared, wide-eyed. What had she gotten herself into? She thought she was here to celebrate an impending wedding.

Kiki reached for a finger sandwich from the triple tiered server. She munched on it mindlessly. I could see the wheels in her brain spinning. "Ashley, you said the police have ruled Candi Cheng's drowning as a homicide. What are they basing that on?"

"Oh, please, girls," Aunt Ruby cried. "This is dear Scarlett's wedding shower. Is this what you want her to remember about this event? Talk of a woman's murder?"

"Aunt Ruby is right," Melanie said. "Shall I pour for each of you?"

"Yes, Melanie, please do," Aunt Ruby responded. "We've got all of this lovely food. Dainty sandwiches and small sweets. Let's try to enjoy ourselves. And after we eat, you can open your presents, Scarlett."

Aunt Ruby to the rescue.

"OK," Jackie said, unable to let go. "We won't speak of murder. But I do have to tell you that Ron had an interesting conversation with one of Citigroup's legal counsel. And they had never heard of an outstanding debt owed by the Bellamy Mansion. There was no such debt. Neither did they have any outstanding notes underwritten by their predecessors that had been submitted by Thaddeus Greensleeves. In fact, according to the files at Citigroup, he doesn't exist."

"Are you saying this was all a scam?" I asked, incredulous.

"Yes," Jackie responded. "A scam. Cooked up by my deceased husband and Han Cheng!"

"There seems to be more than one scam being perpetuated in this town," Melanie declared. "That dreadful Vanessa Holder is suing me for slander. That is all a scam. My lawyer has deposed numerous vendors and has their sworn statements that she demanded two sets of invoices from them: one reflecting the true cost, the other padded for the client. She is finished in this town."

Melanie turned to me. "Ashley, I want you to tell Nick that Vanessa Holder planned and carried out the party that was held at the Bellamy Mansion on New Year's Eve. She was at the mansion the night before Willie was wounded. I think she has something to do with that shooting."

Before I could respond, Scarlett burst out, "Shooting? At the Bellamy Mansion where we are holding the reception?"

Melanie covered her mouth with her hand. "Oh dear lord, I really put my foot in it. I am so sorry, Scarlett."

"You didn't tell me about a shooting," Scarlett cried.

Aunt Ruby to the rescue again. "That is because, dear heart, the gunman has been arrested and incarcerated. He will not be troubling our town again. Now, your reception is going to be peaceful and elegant and fun."

"Yes, Aunt Ruby," Scarlett said docilely. Then she surprised us by bursting out in laughter. "I thought this was such a peaceful, sweet little town. I live right in the heart of bustling Manhattan. But New York City is tame compared to Wilmington!"

I turned to Esther. She was comfortably plump and pretty, wearing a bright pink suit with a pink and white stripped ruffled blouse underneath. An outfit she undoubtedly wore to church.

"Esther," I began, "as the two branches of the Hudson family are now speaking to each other, can you tell us what the feud was about? Do you know?"

Esther chuckled. "Do I know? 'Course, I know. It was over me!"

"You?" I asked.

"Well yes. Suppose I know that. You see, the Hudson boys—my Willie and his brother Abinah—were always competitive. We all met at Williston High School. Willie and I were in the same class. Abinah was a grade above us. Abinah 'liked' me, as we used to say in those days. He began courting me, taking me to dances, bringing me flowers."

She laughed, and fanned her face with a cloth napkin. "At every dance, Willie would cut in. Me oh my, but was he a handsome dude. And so smart…and so loveable. But I was determined to study hard and make good grades, maybe go to college. So I kept them both at arms' length.

"Then Abinah graduated. I remember that summer so well. Like it was just yesterday."

"I know what you mean," Aunt Ruby said. "The days do run together in a rush, don't they, Esther?"

"So what happened next?" I asked Esther.

"Abinah had been admitted to Chapel Hill. And he had his heart set on law school, after undergraduate school. He asked me to wait for him. To be his girl. And we'd date when he came home on school breaks, he said. And he'd write me every day."

"He was gone, and Willie was here," Melanie said knowingly.

"That's right, Melanie. And sure 'nuff, I was partial to Willie. Oh, he'd flash me that big smile of his and just take my breath away. My heart would just go pitty-pat till I thought I would swoon. Swept me off my feet, he did.

"We married right after graduation. And Abinah never forgave us. Neither one of us."

"Not even after he married?" I asked.

"Not even then. Held a grudge for all of their lives. But now he's lost his son. First of the Hudson children to die. And he must be mellowing, having second thoughts.

"I was listening when Willie called Abinah to express his sorrow about Brian's passing. And after a while, those two just started chattering away, catching up on more than fifty years of silence."

"Thank goodness for that," Aunt Ruby said.

"Praise the Lord, I say," Esther finished.

THIRTY-ONE

"Zip me up, Aunt Ruby, please," I asked and lifted my hair off my neck.

Melanie and I were dressing for Scarlett's wedding at my house, taking turns in front of my large, antique cheval looking glass. We had matching dresses, silky and red, and very feminine with deep V necklines and long sleeves. But while Melanie's dress fit her trim figure like a dream, my zipper was stuck.

"Pull harder, Aunt Ruby," I said.

"I'm trying," she said.

"Here, let me," Melanie said, taking hold of the zipper and giving it a yank. "There. That did it."

To Aunt Ruby she said, "Ashley is finally growing breasts, and she needs to buy new clothes."

I studied my figure in the mirror. She was right. There they were. I had boobs. I yawned at my reflection.

"I can't ever seem to get enough sleep," I complained. "No matter how early I go to bed."

Aunt Ruby whirled me around and scrutinized me closely. "Ashley, you have got a look about you. I've seen that look before. A certain softness."

"Oh, that's just because she's getting a lot of good sex," Melanie said. "Jon can't keep his hands off her."

Aunt Ruby sat me down. "Tell me, child. Are your breasts tender?"

"Yes," I said, then blushed. "But I thought that was just because of…you know…"

"Honeymooning," Melanie finished.

"Don't be embarrassed, dear," Aunt Ruby said. "We're all sexual beings. That's the way the good Lord made us.

"Now, tell me, Ashley dear, when was the last time you had a visit from Aunt Flo."

"Aunt Flo?" I asked, bewildered. Who was Aunt Flo? Then I got it. "Oh, you mean…Oh, I'm so irregular, Aunt Ruby, always have been. I don't pay much attention to that."

"Well, when was the last time?" Melanie asked, hands on hips.

"Oh, dear, let's see. Ohmygosh! It has been a while. Since before the wedding. I completely forgot. I got so caught up in the wedding, and then the honeymoon. And then poor Willie getting shot, and all that has been happening here. I just forgot about that.

"It's been…a while. Let's see, almost three months." I drew in my breath sharply. "Oh, Aunt Ruby," I breathed, "does that mean? Melanie? Do you think? Could it be?"

Aunt Ruby got up and embraced me. "Sure looks that way to me, dear girl."

AT ST. JAMES CHURCH I floated down the aisle on a cloud of utter joy. A baby! Aunt Ruby said I was having a baby. I couldn't wait to get to the drug store and buy a pregnancy test kit.

I was contemplating how I might break away between the wedding and the reception and run to the

CVS for a kit as I reached the side altar. Scarlett and Ray's wedding was small and private—just family—and they were marrying at the side altar in the smaller space of the sanctuary. I was smiling like crazy; I could feel my mouth stretching to my cheeks. I smiled at Melanie. I smiled at the minister. I especially smiled at Jon who waited at the altar beside a beaming Ray. Jon gave me a loving wink. I couldn't wait to tell him what Aunt Ruby suspected.

Then the organ segued into Lohengrin and Scarlett appeared. She had on a form fitting ivory lace gown, very Thirties looking, like something Wallace Simpson, the Duchess of Windsor, might have worn. I recalled how there were many really upscale vintage clothing stores in New York City and wondered if Scarlett had bought her gown there. Wherever she had acquired it, she looked absolutely gorgeous in it—it was perfect for her. And she looked so happy.

We were all thrilled with Scarlett's marriage to Ray. Aunt Ruby and Binkie. Cam. And of course Kiki couldn't be happier. She adored Scarlett.

But on the ride to the church with just Aunt Ruby and me, Melanie had expressed that she hated to see a hunk go off the market.

"What?" I had asked. "Off the market? You make it sound like he was for sale."

"I know, I know," she had said, "but suppose you liked Cadillacs and you learned that every Cadillac had been sold, that there was not a single one to be found? Wouldn't you lament the scarcity?"

"But Melanie," I said, as if explaining to a child, "*you* are no longer available."

Melanie had given me a sharp look. "I just mean that hate it when a beautiful man with lots of money is grabbed up and whisked away."

I just looked at Aunt Ruby and shook my head, as to ask, "Is she for real?"

But Aunt Ruby surprised me. "I think I know what you mean, Melanie. I once had a terrible crush on a handsome young man, and then I discovered that he was taken, and would never ask me out. I was devastated. I cried for weeks."

"Who was he, Aunt Ruby?" I asked. I knew nothing about Aunt Ruby's love life, but surely she had had one.

"Well, I don't know if I should say."

"You can trust us, Aunt Ruby," Melanie said. "We're family. We'll never tell, will we, Ashley?"

"No. I won't tell."

"OK then, if you give me your word. It was Rickie Barrett. Scarlett's father. But when he saw your mother, he only had eyes for her.

"And naturally I respected that. Still, you can't just turn off those feelings like turning water off at the tap. It's like Esther Hudson said the other day, he made my heart go pitty-pat.

"A woman can care for a lot of men in her lifetime but the ones that make her heart beat faster are few and far between."

"I know just what you mean," I said, thinking how when I caught a glimpse of Jon my heart started to race.

"And so do I," Melanie said. "Still, I'm not blind.

And I do admire a manly set of shoulders and slim hips!"

We laughed and parked in front of the church.

THIRTY-TWO

THE RECEPTION WAS JUST as we had planned, with a Valentine's heart theme and red and white colors. A tent had been set up in the rear yard of the Bellamy Mansion garden with a buffet and round tables for the guests. The Valentine's theme continued with the menu, the food that Kimberly had planned.

"I sure will miss that girl," Elaine told me as she was refilling the shrimp platter.

"Is she leaving?" I asked.

"Yes," Elaine said. "She found a good job. She's going to work for one of those global corporations in the information technology department."

"Good for her," I said.

Just then Jon caught my hand and led me away. "I need my girl," he told Elaine. "There's dancing on the piazza and they are playing our song."

"At Last" was being played by the DJ Melanie had hired. Jon put his arms around me and started to dance.

"I have something to tell you," I said.

"And I have something to tell you," he said.

"You first," I said.

"Listening to Scarlett and Ray exchange their wedding vows, I thought how grateful I was that you said yes to me. Thank you for marrying me, Ashley. I'll always love you. Always have and I always will."

"Oh, Jon, you touch me to the bottom of my heart."

The music ended. "What did you want to tell me?"

"I have…"

"Come on, you two," Cam called. "The photographer is taking pictures of the bridal party. You're needed inside the mansion. Right away."

"What were you about to say?" Jon asked as we stepped inside the open front door.

I smiled at him. "It can wait, darling. Later."

AFTER THE PHOTOGRAPHS, Ray corralled Cam and Jon and led them out onto the piazza for a man-to-man talk. What was that about, I thought as I watched them huddle, shoulder to shoulder. Melanie was right: there was something to be said for a set of manly broad shoulders and slim hips. But when would I get to tell Jon my exciting news?

I was feeling hungry and now that I suspected I was pregnant, I was not denying myself food. I was eating for two and I would enjoy every bite.

I went down the outside stairs into the garden and into the tent. I filled my plate and carried it over to one of the tables where I had left my purse in a chair.

As I sat down, my cell phone rang inside my purse. I should have turned it off. I retrieved my phone from my purse and saw that someone had been calling me from the same number repeatedly. Must be important.

I answered the phone.

"Ashley, it's Nick. I've been trying to reach you. Don't you ever answer your phone?"

"Not when I'm in a wedding, I don't. When will

you ever learn to be courteous to me?" I asked, mad at myself that I had answered the phone.

"Oh," he said. "Sorry. I forgot all about the wedding. That's today, right? Well, sorry, but I've got some important news for you."

"Can't this wait? I'm at a wedding reception. I'm enjoying myself. Or I was enjoying myself before you called."

"No, it can't wait, Ashley!"

"OK, then shoot. What is so important?" I picked up a shrimp with my fingers and began to nibble.

Kimberly approached my table with a bottle of wine and started to fill my glass. I didn't have time to tell her I wasn't drinking wine anymore.

Nick went on urgently, "We now have the cause of Brian Hudson's death. Remember that cigar you picked up and gave us? We sent it off to the state lab in Raleigh. And it was the cause of death."

"The cigar caused Brian's death!" I exclaimed. "But how?"

"There were oleander seeds imbedded in the tip of the cigar. Brian ingested one of them. Oleander is highly toxic."

"How did oleander seeds get into the cigar?" I asked. "Oh, I get it. You mean someone put them in the cigar. To poison Brian."

Kimberly spilled some of the wine, set the bottle down, and began mopping the spill with a napkin.

"That's exactly what happened," Nick said and explained in a rush, "You know how a smoker clips off the end of the cigar before lighting up. Well, that's because there is a blob of tobacco glued to the mouth end of the cigar to hold the leaves in place. So it's that blob that the smoker is clipping off. Well, someone had tampered with the cigar. Removed the tobacco blob, inserted three oleander seeds into the cigar, then glued the blob back onto the cigar.

"Then Brian, unknowingly, clips off the blob, lights up, sucks in, and sucks one of the seeds into his mouth. And then, without thinking, swallowed it.

"That's what killed him, Ashley. The symptoms fit with oleander poisoning. So, I just wanted you to know and to thank you for being so observant…Wait a minute. Heck, I'm being beeped. I gotta go. Thanks again, Ashley."

And he was gone.

Kimberly was staring at me. And I was staring at her, remembering a scene I had witnessed the night of the party when Brian had collapsed.

My mouth dropped open. "Ahhhh. It was you," I blurted out without thinking. "I saw you passing the box of cigars. I saw you select one and hand it to Brian. But why? Why, Kimberly?"

In answer, she reached under her long black apron and into her pocket. Then she moved the apron and showed me the gun she held in her hand.

"I don't want to hurt you, Ashley, so don't make me." She looked around inside the tent at the guests at their tables. "And I don't want to shoot up this place and hurt a lot of people unnecessarily, so just do as I say."

Involuntarily, my hand went to my stomach. "Kimberly, please, I'm pregnant. Don't hurt me. Tell me what you want. I'll do anything."

"We're going to take a casual walk up the stairs and into the mansion. We'll go up to the third floor. I know just where to stash you."

"I'll go with you," I said. "I'll do anything. Just don't shoot my baby."

"OK, get up and let's go. If anyone stops us, you just say we're going to the bathroom. There's one of the second floor. No one will think anything of it."

Kimberly had changed. She was no longer the shy, eager to please girl.

No one stopped us or even seemed to see us as we went up the stairs to the porch, into the mansion, and directly up to the second floor. Kimberly followed me, her hand under her apron. "I've got this gun trained on you," she warned me, "so don't go doin' anything stupid."

On the second floor we passed one of the guests coming out of the bathroom, but she just said "hey" and went on down.

As we mounted the stairs to the third floor, Kimberly started to talk nervously, as if coaching herself. "I'm all packed. Elaine paid me earlier. Even gave me a tip. Nothing to stop me."

Then to me, "If'n you don't go yellin' or something."

She was dropping her g's, as she had the day I had caught her play acting that she was the lady of the mansion.

"I won't yell," I promised.

"See that you don't and I won't hurt you and that baby. I don't want to hurt you, Ashley. I like you. You and Melanie and Elaine have been good to me. I don't want to hurt none of you. So just shush up and listen."

We were in the upstairs hall now and she was guiding me down the hallway. As if to remind me, there was a baby cradle on display up here.

"You wanted to know why I did it. Well, I'll tell you why. My folks used to live here in Wilmington. You didn't know that, did you? They were one of the early settlers here.

"My ancestors were so clever, they could do most anything to make a livin'. They were good carpenters. And they were good at plumbing, too. They tried to get the job installin' the fancy plumbing in this house. But no, those dang Hudsons underbid them. And they got the job. They were always takin' the work away from my people.

"So my great-granddaddy got fed up, disgusted with this town, and filled with hate for those Hudsons. He just up and left, moved his family to Virginia where they settled for a while. Then after he died, my grand-daddy moved the family west to West Virginia.

"About nineteen hundred the coal mines had started up and there was work. Those mine owners raped the land and treated the miners like dirt, but like my daddy said, the work put food on the table."

We had reached the tank room.

"So this is about revenge?" I said, trying to keep her talking. Was she going to force me into that tank? Oh, no. I hate small spaces. They terrify me.

"Sure is about revenge, and I got mine. Settled the score for my family. I grew up hearing about how the Hudsons took work away from us, destroyed our liveli-hood. So I got even. Got rid of that Brian Hudson. And good riddance. The last thing the world needs is another lawyer. Too bad I missed the old man."

I stared at her. "You? You shot Willie?"

"Sure 'nuff. I'm a crack shot. My daddy used to take me huntin' with him. Taught me how to use a gun and I was a right good marksman. And we didn't hunt for no sport either, like most of those jackasses do. We hunted for the food. We needed that game to keep us fed."

"But what about Candi? She wasn't a Hudson. Why did you kill her?"

"That woman was nasty. Garbage. I was here alone one day, just strollin' around, thinking how nice it would be to live in a house like this. I may have been talking to myself.

"All of a sudden, she appeared. And she started screaming at me. How this was going to be her house. How I was trespassing. She yelled at me to get out. Screaming at me that I was white trash, and wasn't fit to wipe her shoes. Nasty stuff."

Kimberly looked around wildly. "I had this gun in my fanny pack. I told her to shut up and when she wouldn't, I pulled out the gun. I couldn't shoot, too many people would have heard. So I gave her a good whack on the head. Just to shut her up. And then…well, I got carried away. I hit her some more.

"She deserved it. She was evil. And she was such a little bitty thing, I carried her down to the basement and hid her under a tarp in the area way."

She laughed. "People walked by her all day, and didn't even know she was there. After dark, I came back and dumped her into the cistern. I was pushing the slab back over the opening when that security guard showed up, and I had to skedaddle before he saw me."

Kimberly was crazy. I tried to remain calm. "Kimberly, I'm sorry. I can understand how you feel. Just let me go. I won't tell anyone. I promise. This will be our secret. And you'll be far away."

"I can't do that, Ashley. Wish I could, but I can't risk it."

We were alone on the third floor and she had exposed the gun, now pointing it directly at my belly.

"Come on." She stepped over to the tank and reached up to the top to slide the moveable cover to the open position. "Just enough room for you to climb in there. It won't hurt you none to be in there. Someone will find you later. But by then I'll be gone. And I was careful not to tell anyone exactly where I am going."

"Kimberly, please don't make me get in there. I can't stand small spaces. I panic. I have claustrophobia. I'll scream. I won't be able to stop myself."

"Aw, that stuff is just in your head. Now, go on, skedaddle in there." She glared at me, the kid gloves off. "Unless you'd rather I shoot you. Then I'll just shoot anyone who gets in my way. I don't care how many I have to take out. Don't care a bit."

"OK, OK. I'll do it." What choice did I have? I hoisted myself up onto the tank, maneuvered my legs in through the opening, and dropped down inside.

Then it was just like that dream that I'd had in the car. I was the baby inside the trunk and the lid was closing, closing, blocking out the light and the air.

But there was air, I knew that. I was familiar with the construction of the tank, and I knew the sliding door did not fit tight. I had air. I would not suffocate. But then why did I feel like I couldn't breathe?

THIRTY-THREE

I WAS HYPERVENTILATING. Crying, and screaming, and praying all at once. My heart raced.

And then Aunt Ruby's voice spoke clearly inside my head. "Child, you must stop this carrying on for the good of your baby. Now, calm yourself. Jon will find you."

"OK, little one," I spoke to my child. "You and I are in this together. All we have to do is sit tight and wait for Daddy to rescue us."

The inside of the tank was dark and grimy, but a little light and air filtered in. I made myself as comfortable as I could, sat with my back against one side, and my legs stretched out to the other. And I waited. While I waited I said baby names to myself. First girl names, then boy names, then all mixed up.

I had no idea how much time had passed. Then I heard the voice I had been listening for. Jon's voice.

"Ashley! Ashley! Are you up here?"

"Yes," I hollered. But would he hear me? I kicked the side of the tank and sent a shower of grime falling all over me. I kicked again.

Suddenly the tank cover was opening. And then there was Jon's face—Jon's beloved face—looking down at me. "Ashley," he cried, his voice full of fear.

I was able to stand up. My head and shoulders out of the tank. I took a deep breath of clean air. Jon reached for me. And somehow, by sheer will power, lifted me out of the tank. He was in a very awkward position, but between the two of us we got me out.

In a rush, I told him the whole story. "We've got to call Nick," I said. "He's got to find her. She's a psychopath. Who knows how many more people she will kill?"

"But what kind of car does she drive?" Jon asked.

"Elaine will know," I answered.

I SLEPT, AND SLEPT, and slept. At times I'd whimper in my sleep and Jon would reach for me, comfort me, hold me. Sometime in the night, he whispered to me, "Nick called. The state troopers caught her on interstate forty. She was ranting and raving like a lunatic and confessed to everything, even tampering with the belvedere railing."

IN THE MORNING, I woke as Jon carried in a tray with breakfast.

"How are you feeling?" he asked.

"Like new," I said. And realized that was true. One chapter of my life had closed, another had opened. And I knew, deep in my heart, even without a pregnancy test, that I was carrying our baby.

"Our friends and family have been calling all morning. I'm surprised the phone didn't wake you. I told them you were fine but resting. They'll all be over this evening, bringing food."

"Good," I said, "I'm ready to celebrate."

I ate my breakfast with him watching my every move. "Thanks. That was good. I was famished. Now I'm going to take my shower."

"I'll be downstairs working on the computer," Jon said. "Call me if you need your back scrubbed."

I enjoyed my long, warm shower. I washed my hair and dried it. Rubbed on body lotion, sprayed on perfume.

Then I went to the top of the stairs and called down, "Jon! Jon, I need you."

I went over to the bed and reclined on it in what I thought would be a provocative position. I arranged two long silk scarves over my body. One covering my breasts, the other covering my lower abdomen.

Jon stopped just inside the door, surprise registering on his face. Surprise and delight. "What did I do to deserve this?" he asked, grinning from ear to ear.

"Get over here," I said, "and I'll tell you just what you did."

And in two swift strides, he was at my side, then on the bed with me, then stretching out beside me.

I took his hand, lifted it to my lips, and kissed it. Then I placed it on my belly.

"Papa Bear, meet Baby Bear."

REQUEST YOUR FREE BOOKS!

2 FREE NOVELS
PLUS 2 FREE GIFTS!

WORLDWIDE LIBRARY ®
Your Partner in Crime